Steve Taylor was born in Southeast London in 1949. He married his wife, Monica, in 1973 and they moved to Surrey in 1979. They have three grown-up children and four grandchildren who live close by.

Steve is semi-retired and in their free time, Steve and Monica like to travel. Steve also enjoys carpentry and reupholstering antique chairs. This is Steve's first book.

For my three amazing grandsons, Edward, Harry and James, and my beautiful granddaughter, Persie.

Steve Taylor

THE RAINBOW GANG

AUSTIN MACAULEY PUBLISHERS™

LONDON • CAMBRIDGE • NEW YORK • SHARJAH

A CIP catalogue record for this title is available from the British Library.

ISBN 9781528984744 (Paperback)
ISBN 9781528984751 (ePub e-book)

www.austinmacauley.com

First Published (2020)
Austin Macauley Publishers Ltd
25 Canada Square
Canary Wharf
London
E14 5LQ

With thanks to Monica Taylor, Hannah Rogan, Barry Taylor and Chris Taylor for their continuous encouragement and support throughout the writing of this book. With grateful thanks to Austin Macauley for believing in me and making this dream come true.

Chapter 1

Charlie White woke up early. His younger brother, Freddie, was still asleep in his own bedroom. Downstairs, he could hear his mum and dad chatting, hopefully making breakfast.

Charlie thought about yesterday. It had been his birthday; he was now 10 years old. He had had a really great day with his best friends: Jack, Robbie, Billy, Billy's twin sister, Sophie and his own brother Freddie.

Together, they were known as the 'Rainbow Gang'. They'd had this name since they were little. Charlie and Freddie's surname is White. Jack's surname is Green, Robbie's surname is Black and Billy and Sophie's surname is Jackson, but they both have red hair and so are included in the gang!

They had all been to the leisure centre and had tried the rock-climbing wall. It was fantastic! He was the first to climb all the way to the top; the instructor said he was a natural. Even Freddie managed to get to the top, as did all the others. After the rock wall, they all went back to Charlie and Freddie's house where they ate pizza and chips, except for Freddie who does not like pizza so he had a sandwich. Charlie opened the presents his friends had bought him: two Lego kits and some DVDs. They then played in the garden.

Charlie thought it was the best birthday ever. Mum and Dad had given him a new bike; he was getting too big for his old one and Freddie was getting too big for his bike so he now had Charlie's old one. Freddie is really pleased!

"Charlie," Mum called, "are you up yet?"

"Yes Mum."

"Do you want breakfast?"

"Yes, please."

"Wake Freddie up and come downstairs."

"OK."

Charlie went in and poked his brother who sat up looking worried. "What's up?" asked Charlie.

"I was dreaming and, in my dream, someone had stolen my new bike—your old bike. We couldn't find it anywhere."

"Don't worry," said Charlie, "Both our bikes are locked up in Dad's shed; they're safe in there. Come on, get up, Mum's making breakfast."

Charlie and a sleepy Freddie went downstairs to the kitchen; Mum and Dad were both there.

"Do you want toast, cereal or something else?" asked Mum.

"Can I have boiled egg and soldiers, please?" asked Freddie.

"Yes, can I have the same please, Mum?"

"OK, sit down; it will be a few minutes."

"What are you going to do today, boys?" said Dad.

"Can we go to the park on our bikes?" asked Charlie.

Charlie and Freddie are lucky boys: their garden backed onto the park and like a lot of other houses, they had a gate in the garden that led straight into the park.

It is a lovely open space with a playground, a small kids' splash pool, a five-a-side football pitch, a cricket pitch and two tennis courts and just recently, a set of outdoor exercise machines for the grownups was installed, which of course, all the kids tried out!

There is also a pavilion and a hut. The groundsman is Mr Jackson, a local man who seems to know everyone. He is Billy and Sophie's dad. It is always quite busy at the park, especially at the weekend.

After breakfast, Charlie and Freddie went into the garden and unlocked the padlock on Dad's shed. Much to Freddie's relief, both bikes were still there; both boys found cloths and started to polish their bikes.

Charlie pulled at another pile of rags and stopped when a strange wooden box was revealed.

"Freddie," said Charlie, "look at this!"

"What is it?" asked Freddie.

"I don't know, but I've never seen it in here before."

"It must be Dad's," Freddie decided.

"But there's normally just a pile of boxes and tins there and where are they now?"

"Let's go and ask Dad," said Freddie.

"Let's just have a quick look at the box," said Charlie as he pulled the box to the middle of the shed.

The box was made of wood about the size of a typical pirate's treasure chest, except with a flat top. It had a lid on and what looked like a handle on the top but it was sunk into the lid. Around the edge of the lid, were buttons with the letters of the alphabet.

The box looked very old; it had carvings all over it—trees, animals, strange creatures and what seemed to be small figures and much bigger ones.

"Go on then, Charlie, open it up and let's have a look inside," said Freddie excitedly.

"OK, but what do you think might be inside?"

"Don't know, open it!"

Charlie grabbed two sides of the lid and lifted. It would not budge; he tried the other two sides, still nothing. Freddie leant over and tried to help. Still no movement.

"What was it that that Ali Baba man said in the story?" asked Freddie.

"Open something," said Charlie.

"Open sesame seeds."

"Nearly right."

"It's 'open sesame'," said Charlie.

"OK, 'open sesame'."

The boys waited, taking it in turns to say 'open sesame' but it did not open.

Freddie said, "It must be locked."

"Can you see a keyhole? No! And anyway, we don't have a key or hadn't you noticed?" sneered Charlie.

"What about if we spelled out 'open sesame' on the letter buttons?" Freddie suggested.

"Freddie, you're a genius!" Charlie exclaimed.

Charlie pressed 'O', Freddie pressed 'P', Charlie pressed 'E' and Freddie pressed 'N'.

Charlie was about to press 'S' for sesame when there was a quiet click and the handle at the top of the box silently slid up.

"Wow!" said Freddie, "That's really cool."

"We only had to spell 'open'," laughed Charlie.

The boys sat silently looking at the box.

Chapter 2

Mr and Mrs White were busy in the kitchen; Mrs White was finishing the tidying up.

Mr White had loaded the dishwasher and was making another cup of coffee.

"The boys are quiet down at the shed," said Mrs White.

"They're probably cleaning their bikes again. I don't suppose they will keep that up for long! Still, they're not under our feet so leave them to it; we've got to go shopping soon. I'll give them a shout when we leave."

In the shed, Charlie and Freddie still sat staring at the box. "Let's open it then, Charlie," Freddie said.

"OK," said Charlie.

Standing up, he leant over the box and with both hands, gripped the handle and gently eased the lid from the box. It made a noise like someone drawing air between their lips. Charlie put the lid on the floor.

The boys peered into the now open box.

There were several things inside. What appeared to be a wooden mallet? Not like Dad's one on the bench, it looked as though it was made from a bit of a tree trunk with a bit sticking out of one side, like a handle. It looked very old.

Charlie reached in and picked it up. It was not heavy but very hard and the handle bit was very shiny.

Freddie leant across and took the mallet from his brother. He knocked it on the shed floor; it did not make a noise at all.

The brothers looked at each other in amazement.

Freddie dropped the mallet—no noise again.

Charlie took the mallet and tried hitting it on the floor—nothing! He hit harder, still no noise. He tried hitting it on other things but it still made no sound. He put it down, gently.

"This is very odd," said Charlie.

"It's a bit scary," said Freddie.

"Charlie, Freddie," Dad called.

Suddenly, the mallet flew into the box and the lid shot up on top and the box slid to one side. It became a pile of small tins and boxes and bits of rags. A strange voice from under the boxes and tins said, "Don't tell your dad."

The boys looked at each other with their mouths wide open.

"Are you boys still in the shed?" called Dad.

Quick as a flash, the boys grabbed their bikes and wheeled them outside.

"You've been very quiet; what have you been doing?" asked Dad.

"We've been polishing our bikes."

"OK then. Mum and I are going to the supermarket. We'll only be about half an hour; are you going into the park and is Robbie going with you?"

"Yes, we'll call for Robbie when we go through the gate."

"OK, have you got your backdoor key?"

"Yes," said Charlie.

"Let Mrs Black know what you're up to and look after Freddie."

"Will do, Dad, see you later."

"See you later, Dad," said Freddie.

"Okay, be good," said Dad.

The boys left their bikes by the gate to the park. They listened until they heard Mum and Dad drive away. They ran back to the shed and opened the door to find the box in the middle of the floor.

"Wow," said Freddie, "This is really weird."

"I know," said Charlie, "Where did that voice come from?"

"Don't know. Do you think we should open the box again?"

Charlie sat for a long while, thinking. Freddie just sat staring at the box.

"It isn't dangerous, Charlie, is it? It only said not to tell Dad. Was it a warning or was it just advice? Is it secret? Where did it come from? What's it for?"

"Hold on, Freddie, that's too many questions and I don't know the answer to any of them, but I think it's exciting," replied Charlie. "Come on, let's open it again."

"OK," said Freddie, "let me do it."

"Go on then."

Freddie pushed the 'OPEN' buttons and like before, the handle popped up. Charlie lifted the lid off.

The mallet was lying there among the other things. Charlie lifted it and tried hitting it on the floor again...no noise. He put it gently on the floor.

"What are the other things in there?" asked Freddie.

"Let's have a look then," said Charlie.

"Well, I think I know what this is but I've never seen one made out of wood," said Charlie.

"What is it then?" asked Freddie.

"I think it's a compass."

"It can't be; we use compasses at school to draw circles."

"Not that sort of compass. This type shows you where north, south, east and west are."

"Oh, I know," said Freddie.

Charlie lifted the compass out of the box. Just like the box, it was carved in a very detailed way.

"OK Charlie, let's see it work," said Freddie.

"You don't have to do much; just hold it level and the needle will turn until it points to the north," said Charlie, holding the compass flat on the palm of his hand.

"That's really clever," said Freddie, "So north is straight down the garden."

"Yes, but on and on in a straight line through the park, through the woods and all the way to the North Pole."

"Wow," said Freddie, "That's a really long way."

"It is, but what's a compass in the box for?"

"What's any of it for; what's that funny-looking thing with straps on?"

"Don't know," said Charlie, lifting it out.

"It looks like a belt with another belt attached… What's that metal bit on the front?" said Freddie.

"It looks like a sort of small eggcup with a lid on it. Perhaps you put things in it and look, there's a little spike in the bottom bit. I wonder what that's for."

"Charlie, look! There's a key in the box!"

Chapter 3

Robbie Black lives two doors away from Charlie and Freddie; his back garden also has a gate into the park.

"Are you meeting Charlie and Freddie today?" asked Mrs Black.

"Yes, they said they'd call for me this morning. I thought they'd be here by now. I'll go and call for them instead."

"OK," said Mrs Black, "But let me know what you are going to do. I saw Carol and Mike (Mr and Mrs White) drive off a minute ago so I'll be the one in charge."

"OK Mum, I'll go now."

Robbie left home, walked down the garden, took his bike, went through his gate and turning left, went to Charlie and Freddie's gate. It was unlocked and he went in. No sign of his friends so he called out.

"Charlie, are you home?"

Charlie had only just picked up the key from the box when Robbie called out; the box did not react to Robbie's voice.

Charlie still held the key and opened the shed door.

"Quick Robbie, come in," he said.

Robbie stepped into the shed.

"What's going on, Charlie?" he asked.

"Look what we've found," said Freddie, pointing to the box.

"What is it and what are these things?"

"We don't really know how the box got here and we don't understand what some of the bits are for but watch this."

Charlie picked up the mallet and hit it on the floor. As usual, there was no noise. Robbie looked shocked. He opened his mouth but no words came out.

Freddie said, "It's magic."

Charlie thought for a minute. "You know, Freddie, I think you are right; it is magic."

"I don't get it," Robbie said at last. "Let's have a go with the hammer thing."

"It's a mallet," Charlie said, passing it to Robbie.

Robbie held the mallet, turning it round in his hand. He then gently tapped it on the shed floor. No noise. He tried hitting several different things, all the time his mouth opening wider and wider. He dropped the mallet on the floor.

"That's weird!" he exclaimed.

"We know, and there are other things in the box. A compass, this thing," Charlie said holding up the strap thing, "and also this key we just found, which is made of wood."

Charlie passed the key to Robbie.

"It's very old-looking and feels very hard; where does it fit?"

"We've only just found it so we don't know."

"Is there anything else in the box?" asked Robbie.

"Let's see, there's a coil of rope here too," Charlie said, taking the rope from the box and holding it up.

"That's quite a lot," said Freddie.

"How long is it?" asked Robbie.

Charlie stood up and got his dad's tape measure. They went outside and unravelled the rope. Charlie pulled out the tape; the rope measured exactly 16 feet or 4.877 metres.

"That's a lot of rope. What's it for?" said Robbie.

"Who knows?" Charlie said, winding the rope.

He did not do a very good job but he did not need to—the rope automatically wound itself up into neat coils.

"That's really cool," said Freddie.

"It's freaking me out," Robbie said, sitting down on the grass.

"Let's think about this," said Robbie. "What have you got so far?"

"Well, a box that can appear and disappear, an old wooden key but no keyhole, an old wooden compass, a rope that can coil itself up and a strappy eggcup thing."

"Can we have another look in the box?"

In the shed, the box was still there but the lid was back in place.

"How does the lid come off?"

"By pressing the button things on the sides to spell 'OPEN'." Charlie pressed the buttons and lifted the lid off.

"Oh, and another thing, the box spoke to us."

"What!" exclaimed Robbie.

"It spoke to us; it said, 'don't tell your dad'."

"You're kidding."

"No, but that's all it has said so far."

Suddenly, the inside of the box lit up. The three friends looked in. There was now a keyhole at the bottom of the box.

"That wasn't there before," said Freddie, "was it?"

"I don't think so but it's quite dark or it was before that light came on. The insides of the box are just glowing."

"Look," said Freddie, "what's that in the corner?"

Charlie reached in and picked up a small roundish thing.

"It's an acorn," shouted Robbie.

"You're right," agreed Charlie.

"An acorn?" said Freddie, "What can that be for?"

"Don't know. Let's try the key in the keyhole."

It fitted. Charlie slowly turned it. There was a sharp click. Charlie lifted the key and the bottom of the box came with it.

"It's a secret compartment," Freddie said excitedly.

"There's more stuff in there!" Robbie almost shouted.

There was a small pouch, another eggcup strappy thing and what looked like coins.

"Is that money?" asked Freddie.

Charlie picked up the coins and counted them. There were 15.

"Let's have a look," said Freddie and Robbie at the same time.

All three boys studied a coin each. They looked like money, they decided, but not like any money they had seen before. On the front of the coins were pictures of trees but all different. On the back, there were pictures of frogs or fish!

"These are the weirdest coins I've ever seen!" said Charlie.

"Me too," said Robbie.

"And me," agreed Freddie.

"What's in the pouch?" asked Robbie. "Let's have a look."

Charlie lifted out the pouch, opened the top and tipped the contents into his hand.

"It's more acorns," he said.

"Why are there all these acorns?" asked Freddie, "What are they for?"

"We'll have to find out somehow. Come on; Mum and Dad will be back soon. Let's put everything away and go to the park."

Suddenly, all the contents jumped back into the box just as they were before. The box slid back where it came from and magically became a pile of tins, boxes and rags.

"Wow," said Robbie, "that's brilliant."

The three friends went outside, took their bikes and went through the gate and out into the park.

Chapter 4

As the boys entered the park, they could see their friends, Billy and Sophie Jackson and Jack Green, who were over by the pavilion talking to Billy and Sophie's dad.

"The other groundsmen and I are a bit worried about some of the really big old trees," Mr Jackson was saying as Charlie, Freddie and Robbie rode up.

"Hello," he said to the boys, "I was just explaining about how we are worried about some of the trees."

"Why, what's wrong?" the boys said in unison.

"Dad thinks they aren't getting any water at all from the soil," said Sophie.

"If you look at the leaves on all the trees, they're all changing colour like in the autumn. If we'd had a really hot summer and a drought, I could perhaps understand it, but we haven't. It hasn't been particularly hot this year, has it?" asked Mr Jackson.

"No," the group all agreed.

"It's the same with the trees in the woods, look!" Mr Jackson was right: most of the trees were all looking a bit sad.

"What's going to happen?" asked Robbie.

"Well, we've got some scientists coming to investigate. Once they've found the cause, they'll let us know what to do," Mr Jackson said. "Don't worry; we'll sort it out. Off you go and enjoy yourselves."

"See you later, Dad," said Billy and Sophie.

"See you, bye!" said the rest of the boys.

The Rainbow Gang all cycled over to the playground. They laid their bikes down.

Robbie asked Charlie, "Are you going to tell them about 'you know what'?"

"Well, I'm going to have to now, aren't I!"

"Sorry, I wasn't thinking," said Robbie.

"What's he talking about?" asked Jack.

"Freddie and I found something in Dad's shed!"

"What is it?" Sophie asked excitedly.

"Come on, tell us," said Billy.

"Yeah, go on; spill the beans," said Jack.

"OK," said Charlie, "but it's got to stay a secret. We found a really old-looking box; it's got letters and other stuff all over it," added Freddie.

"What else?" asked Billy.

Charlie then told his friends how they found the box. He told them everything else about it. How they had opened it, how it disappears, all the bits inside, the light and how it spoke to them.

Billy, Sophie and Jack just stared at the others. "It's a joke, right?" said Jack.

"No its not," shouted Freddie.

"Alright Freddie, calm down," said Charlie.

"We'll take you and show you, but not yet. If we all pile into our dad's shed, he'll wonder what's going on."

"So when can we see it?" asked Sophie.

"Yeah, I can't wait to see this magic box," Jack said sarcastically.

"We're not making it up, Jack," Charlie said, "I know it sounds weird but honestly, it's all true."

"OK," said Billy, "How are we going to get to see it?"

"We'll have to go to the shed when our mum and dad aren't around."

"What about tomorrow after school? Your mum and dad work and you go to Billy and Sophie's until later."

"Good idea," said Billy. "We usually go out to play in the park anyway!"

"OK," said Jack, "Robbie and I will meet you outside Billy's gate about half past three."

"OK, we'll all meet at half past three," agreed Charlie. "But you can't tell anybody else about the box or its secrets. I don't think we know all about the box. I'm sure it will show us some more stuff. We don't know about the things that we've seen already. Think about what we've told you. A compass, a mallet, two strappy eggcup things, some things that look like coins, a rope, acorns and a key. Then there's the light, the buttons on the lid and the voice. I don't know what it's all about."

Robbie said, "Perhaps, we should try spelling some other words on the buttons."

"OK," said Charlie, "Any other suggestions?"

"Have you tried talking back to the box?" said Jack.

"No, but that's a good idea! What questions could we ask?" said Freddie.

"Well, there's lots," said Charlie, "Like where do you come from? Whose box is it? What are the different items for?"

"Yeah," said Jack, "What's that rope for?"

"And what are those funny strappy things for?" said Freddie.

"OK, so there are lots of questions," said Robbie.

"Yes, so when we meet tomorrow, we will have to decide what we ask but it's no good all blurting out questions at the same time," Charlie said. "We don't even know whether it will work, do we?"

"Maybe we should try asking questions using the buttons first," said Jack.

"OK, but we'll have to decide in advance," Charlie said.

"I think you should decide; it's your box, Charlie… Yours and Freddie's," Sophie said.

"Well, Charlie saw it first and he's older so I suppose it could be his, but I saw it second," muttered Freddie.

"It's ours!" said Charlie, "I'm really looking forward to seeing your faces tomorrow when you see the box for the first time," Charlie said to Billy, Sophie and Jack.

"I can't wait," said Jack.

"Neither can we," said Billy and Sophie at the same time.

"You often say things at the same time," Charlie said.

"Yeah, we know, Mum and Dad say it's a twin thing," said Billy.

"You didn't say that together," Freddie pointed out.

"It would be really weird if we did, Fred," said Sophie.

"Don't call me 'Fred'; you know I don't like it."

"Sorry," said Sophie. "I only do it in fun."

"I know but I still don't like it."

"OK, sorry Fred, oops! I mean Freddie," teased Sophie.

"Come on, let's go to the playground!" Charlie said.

Chapter 5

At exactly 3.30 on Monday afternoon, the Rainbow Gang met at Billy and Sophie's park gate.

"We've told our mum that we will all be in Charlie and Freddie's garden so she knows where we are," said Sophie.

"OK, let's go," Charlie said, leading the way.

They all filed into the garden and Charlie unlocked the shed. They all moved at once to go in.

"Hold on," Charlie said, "let me and Freddie move our bikes out so that there's more room."

The brothers moved their bikes out to the garden.

Robbie, Jack, Sophie and Billy pushed into the shed.

"Where is it?" asked Jack, looking all around. "I can't see any box."

Before he could finish, just as Charlie and Freddie entered the shed, the pile of tins, boxes and rags suddenly became the box.

"There you are," said Charlie, "That's the box."

"It must be magic," said Sophie, "What else could it be?"

Jack moved towards the box and turned it around, revealing all the pictures carved into the sides. "It looks really old," he said.

"Open it up!" shouted Billy.

"Here we go," said Charlie. He pressed the buttons to spell 'OPEN'. There was a click and the handle slid up. Charlie lifted the lid off the box. It looked empty.

"There's nothing in it now," said Freddie. "Charlie, what's going on?"

"It's not empty, look, there's a folded piece of paper in the corner!" Charlie said as he reached in and slowly unfolded the paper.

He read the four words printed on the sheet:
'WELCOME, THE RAINBOW GANG'.

"Show us, does it really say that?" asked Robbie.

"That's all it says," said Charlie, showing it to his friends.

"What's happened to all the other stuff you told us about?" asked Jack.

"I don't know; I don't understand."

"Shall we try asking questions?" suggested Sophie.

"OK, but I feel a bit silly talking to a box," said Charlie.

Suddenly, a light shone from inside, really brightly.

A voice whispered, "I'm a chest, not a box." All six children moved backwards, bumping into the rest of the contents of the shed.

"Sorry," muttered Charlie.

"I'm the Magic Chest."

"Where have you come from?" said Billy.

"I was sent here by Charlie and Freddie's granddad Ron. Now that you are ten years old, you are the Keeper of the Chest."

"But, why me?"

"As you've reached the age of ten, this chest—me—has been transferred from Granddad Ron to you. It's what happens; when you have a ten-year-old grandchild, it will transfer to him or her."

"So, is this really magic?" asked Sophie.

"Of course, you are talking to a chest, aren't you? But wait a minute, I'm talking to you and I don't know who you are. If you spell your names out on the letters on my lid, I'll remember who you are."

"Me first," said Jack.

"Ladies first," said the chest.

Sophie leant forward and spelt out her name. "Hello, Sophie," said the chest.

"Have you got a name?" asked Billy.

"Who are the last two?"

Robbie and Jack spelt their names. "Hello, Robbie and Jack."

"Go on then, tell us your name," said Robbie.

"I actually have two names: one very old one, Alphrick, and quite a new one, Chester."

"You're a chest and your name is Chester?" laughed Charlie.

"Yes, one of the previous keepers of the chest—me, that is—had difficulty saying Alphrick and started calling me Chester, which I liked so now that's my name."

"I can't believe we're sitting here talking to a chest," said Jack.

"So if my granddad Ron was a keeper of the chest, where does he think you are now?" asked Charlie.

"He was only my keeper for five years up to the age of 15. After that, I went to another keeper. I move around every five years, going from keeper to keeper."

"But if Granddad Ron stopped being your keeper when he was 15, how did he know to pass it on to me when I wasn't even born then!"

"We keep in contact," said Chester.

"How can you remember all the keepers if you move on every five years? There must have been loads and loads," said Freddie.

"But what do you do and what do the keepers do?" asked Sophie.

"We work together to keep your world working as it should."

"But the keepers are only kids so how can they help?" Charlie asked.

"That's why there's a chest. My equipment and knowledge lets them do what has to be done."

"Why can't grownups do the work or whatever?"

"They don't fit," said the chest.

"What do you mean?" asked Jack.

"They are too big."

"Too big for what?" said Charlie.

"You'll find out on your first adventure!"

"What do you mean?" asked Freddie this time.

"Close me up. Charlie and Freddie's mum and dad are on their way home. You'd better be out playing in the park when they get here. We'll meet again tomorrow." Charlie put the lid back on Chester the chest, pressed 'CLOSE' on the buttons and as before, the chest magically became the tins and boxes again.

"Come on," said Charlie, "Let's go in the park. We've got to talk about this."

The gang all raced through the gate and rode over to the playground. Sitting in a circle, nobody spoke for a short time, then everybody started talking at once.

"Wait, wait!" said Charlie, "We've got to be organised!"

"Let's make a list of questions that we need to ask Chester," said Sophie.

"Well, I think question number one should be 'what are the contents of Chester for?'" said Charlie. Sophie had taken a pencil and pad out of her small backpack.

"Right, got that, what's next?" she said.

"How about when can we go on our first adventure?" said Freddie.

"Good one," said Robbie.

"Yeah, but how can we go on an adventure? Our parents wouldn't let us go," said Jack.

"That's true," said Billy, "Perhaps that's a question to ask."

"That's three questions so far," said Sophie.

"Will it be dangerous?" said Freddie.

"That's four," said Sophie, jotting it down.

"I wouldn't think Chester would let us do anything dangerous, do you?" said Charlie, "We're only kids."

"Yeah and we're able to go where adults won't fit," said Robbie. "Where can that be?"

"Is that question number five?" asked Sophie.

"Not yet; let's ask if we'll all go. It might only be Charlie and perhaps Freddie; after all, Charlie is the new Keeper," said Billy.

"OK, let's make that question five," Sophie said.

"No, make that number one and alter the rest. We want to go together, don't we?" said Charlie. The rest of them agreed.

"What's the time?" asked Robbie.

Jack looked at his watch. "It's 5 o'clock," he said. "I told my mum and dad I'd be home now. I've got to go."

"Me too," said Robbie.

"OK," said Billy, "We four should go back to our house. We'll see you on the way to school tomorrow."

"See you," they all said.

"Remember, don't tell anyone any of this, OK?" said Charlie.

"OK," the others said.

Chapter 6

On the way to school, the gang huddled together and agreed to meet again outside Billy and Sophie's gate at 3.30.

Later on the way home, everyone agreed that it seemed to be a very long day; they all just wanted to get back to the shed and see Chester.

Billy, Sophie, Charlie and Freddie arrived at the Jackson house just as Mr Jackson came home.

"Have the scientists been to check the trees in the park yet, Dad?" asked Sophie.

"No, not yet," said Mr Jackson, "It's not only our local trees that are affected. It's happening all over the county. It's quite serious. I was watching the TV earlier and they were saying that the aquifers, which are layers of rock underground that hold water, might be losing the water."

"What can they do about it, Dad?" asked Sophie.

"They're not sure. They are going to drill holes and conduct all sorts of tests.

We'll have to wait and see. Anyway, I'll keep you informed so don't worry."

"Anybody fancy a snack?" asked Mrs Jackson.

"What have you got?" asked Billy, "Something quick; we've got to meet Jack and Robbie soon."

"Well, I've made sandwiches so you can take some with you if you want."

"Thanks, Mum," said Billy.

"Yes, thanks, Mrs Jackson," said Charlie.

"Come on, Charlie and Freddie, I think you know me well enough to call me Emma by now."

"Yes, and you can call me Dave."

"Thanks, Emma; thanks, Dave," said Freddie.

"Freddie," said Charlie, "don't be cheeky."

"It's alright; we'd like you both to use our names. It makes us feel younger," said Mrs Jackson.

"It'll seem funny," said Charlie.

"Well, when you're ready."

"OK, thanks, Emma," said Charlie. Everyone laughed.

The four friends grabbed a sandwich each and went into the garden.

"The kids all seem quite excited about something," said Mrs Jackson.

"Yes, well, let's hope that it stops them worrying about this tree problem.

For kids, they seem pretty concerned."

"I can't believe you called my mum Emma," said the twins together.

"Well, she did say," said Charlie.

"I like it," said Freddie. "It's like having two more friends." They all laughed. Outside in the park, Robbie and Jack were already there.

"What are you laughing about?" asked Robbie.

"Oh! Just messing about with Mum and Dad," said Sophie.

"Hurry up," said Jack. "I want to start asking Chester questions." The gang filed into the shed. To the amazement of everyone, Chester was already in the middle of the shed. His lid was off and all the contents were neatly laid out.

"Hello Sophie, hello boys," Chester said.

"Hello," they all replied.

"As you can see, all my bits and pieces are here for us all to look at. I'll explain what they are for," Chester said. "What's this?" he asked as the compass floated up from the floor.

"A compass," they all said.

"Good," said Chester.

"Is it very old?" asked Charlie.

"Yes, it's hundreds and hundreds of years old."

"Where did it come from?" asked the twins together. The other boys all smiled.

"You're doing it again," Freddie said.

"It's because they are twins," said Chester.

"We know, but it's just funny," said Freddie.

"I suppose," said Sophie.

"Chester, what are these things?" asked Freddie, pointing to the strappy eggcup things.

"Charlie, pick one up and see if it will fit round your head." Charlie tried a couple of times and finally did it. One strap went round his head with the other strap over the top of his head. "OK, got it," said Charlie, "What's this cup bit on the front for?"

"Can you open it?" asked Chester. Charlie reached up and fiddled with a small catch and it suddenly opened up.

"OK," said Chester, "Take one of the acorns and push it on to the little spike at the bottom and close the top." Charlie inserted the acorn and as he closed the top, the acorn glowed like a lightbulb.

"That's wicked," said Jack.

"Wicked? I think it's really good," said Chester.

"Sorry," said Jack, "When we say 'wicked', we mean that it's really good."

"Oh," said Chester, "OK, it's wicked, I think!"

The children all laughed.

"Right, we'd better carry on."

"Excuse me," said Freddie.

"Yes?" replied Chester.

"Are you a person as well as a chest?" The shed became very quiet.

"Well, actually, yes, I am."

"But why are you here as a chest?" asked Robbie.

"Our bodies aren't capable of travelling so our minds travel in chests."

"So is your head in the chest somewhere?" asked Freddie.

"Don't be daft, Freddie, don't you think we'd have seen it by now?" said Charlie.

"Charlie's right, Freddie, but my mind is the chest; I'm part of it!"

"OK, it's all magic," said Sophie.

"You're right, Sophie, it is magic."

"OK," said Charlie, "What are the other things for?"

"Yes, let's get back to the other things."

The compass slowly floated up from the floor again.

"You all know what this is; it's a compass.

You know how to use one?" asked Chester. The gang all nodded.

"Yes," they all said.

"Good, you'll be using it soon."

The neatly coiled rope was the next to float up.

"You'll use this rope to measure things," explained Chester.

"What things?" asked Freddie.

"Trees, mainly."

"Trees?" they all asked together.

"Yes, trees," replied Chester. "I'll explain shortly."

The other acorn headlight floated up along with the pouch of acorns.

"You already knew about the bean lights. We'll have to get some more of these, one for each of you."

"Wow, that'll be really cool. One each," said Jack.

"Well, they don't get hot," said Chester.

"Sorry, that's another word we sometimes use to mean good or useful or clever," explained Jack.

"I see, I think," said Chester.

"You said bean lights but they're acorns, not beans," said Freddie.

"You're right of course, Freddie, but where you are going, they are called tree beans. You'll find out soon," said Chester.

The coins floated up next. "Is that money?" asked Billy.

"Yes, it is; you'll need that soon too."

"What about the mallet?" said Robbie. As he said it, the mallet rose from the floor as if it understood. It spun round as if looking at the children.

"The mallet is very important," said Chester, "It has many uses and it has a name, Woody." As Chester said Woody, the mallet spun round to face him. "See?" Chester said, "He knows his name."

"Why doesn't it make any noise when you hit things with it?" asked Charlie.

"It will when you hit the right things. I'll tell you soon and then you'll hear it make noise," Chester smiled. Without warning, from inside Chester, an old-looking brown leather backpack floated up. "Charlie, gather up all the bits and put them in the rucksack," said Chester.

"That's what my granddad calls them," said Robbie. "We call them backpacks."

"Oh yes, I've heard them called that before," Chester remembered. "OK Charlie, put them in the backpack. Now, I want you to go to the park. I want you to look for a big tree. A tree that the rope will reach round. It has to be big enough so that the two ends just meet or not meet but the ends must not overlap," Chester said.

"Does it matter what tree it is?" asked Freddie.

"Not really," said Chester, "But it must be big enough."

"Then what do we do?" asked Charlie.

"Using the compass, find which side of the tree faces north. When you've done that, take Woody out and knock him three times on the north side of the tree. Then just wait. Off you go then!" said Chester, "Your adventure starts now!"

Chapter 7

The gang grabbed their bikes and raced off to the far end of the park nearest to the woods. They decided that the biggest trees were there. They stopped by what they thought was the biggest tree, a very old oak tree. They knew it was an oak because there were acorns all over the grass below it.

"Well, I think we agree that this is a big tree, don't we?" said Charlie.

"Quick, get the rope out!" said Billy.

Charlie removed the backpack and took out the neatly coiled rope. "You take this end and I'll take the other." The two friends walked in opposite directions around the tree. When they met, the two ends were about six inches apart. "This is the right size," said Charlie. The other gang members all agreed that it was the tree.

"OK," said Jack, "Get Woody out."

"Not yet, we've got to find out which is the north side," said Sophie.

"Oh yeah," said Jack, "Charlie, get out the compass."

Charlie reached in the backpack and brought out the compass. He placed it on the palm of his hand. The needle turned and pointed towards the woods.

"Someone's coming," said Robbie. Everyone turned around. Two boys were cycling towards them. Magically, the rope and the compass flashed back into the backpack.

"Oh no," said Sophie, "It's Danny and Jake." Danny Philips and Jake Hutton were cousins. Both were 12 years old and thought they are tough. They were not very popular with most of the other kids in the area. They skidded to a halt, spraying up loads of acorns in the direction of the gang.

"Look Jake, it's the 'Rainbow Gang'," said Danny sarcastically.

"What are you lot doing all the way over here?" said Jake.

"Just looking at the trees," said Sophie.

"What's so interesting about the trees?" said Danny.

"Well, our dad says they're not very well," Sophie replied.

"What, have they got a cold?" said Jake, laughing at his silly joke.

"Not that you two would notice, but the trees seem to be dying," said Billy.

"Well, we do 'cos they spoke about it in school," sneered Danny. "Anyway, I'd have thought your dad 'the groundsman' would be able to fix them!"

"It's more serious than you think. It's not just the trees here but all over the place," said Charlie.

"Who cares?" said Jake, "They're only trees."

"Only trees?" said Jack, "What are you, stupid? Don't you know that trees produce oxygen and without trees, the air would be difficult to breathe?"

"Don't call me stupid," said Jake walking towards Jack. Although Jack was two years younger than the cousins, he was as big as them.

"You don't scare me, Jake," said Jack, "Just go away!"

Danny said, "Pack it in, Jake; you know if you get in trouble again, your dad said he'd ground you all summer."

"Lucky for you, Green," sneered Jake and threw an acorn at Jack. He missed.

"Anyway, what's in the tatty old backpack, Charlie?" asked Danny.

"Yeah, let's have a look," said Jake as he snatched it up off the ground.

"Leave it alone!" shouted Freddie, jumping at Jake.

"There must be something important in there," said Danny. "Let's take a look." He tipped the rucksack upside down and the contents fell on the ground. Four pre-packed ham sandwiches, a packet of salt and vinegar crisps, a bottle of water, a banana and a frisbee.

"Just snacks," said Charlie. "Help yourself if you're that hungry." Everyone laughed except Danny and Jake. Jake threw the bag at Charlie who caught it.

"Come on Danny, let the losers eat their snacks," said Jake. The cousins rode off leaving the gang laughing. When the two were far enough away not to be able to hear them, the gang all started talking at once:

"How did that happen?"

"Where did the rope and other stuff go?"

"That was funny."

"What do we do now?"

"Look," said Sophie. All the bits had disappeared. Freddie picked up the backpack and opened it up.

"All our adventure stuff is in here," he shouted. The gang all looked. Freddie was right, it was all back.

"Right," said Charlie, "We know this tree is big enough and that north is the side facing the woods."

"Go on then Charlie, hit it three times with Woody," said Robbie.

Charlie took Woody out of the backpack. He held it in his right hand and hit it into the palm of his left hand. It still made no noise. He tried a few swings to practice, then stepped up to the tree and gave it three quick hits. *Bang! Bang! Bang!* The noise was so loud that all of the friends jumped back. "Crikey," said Billy, "Everyone in the park must have heard that." They all looked around; no one in the park seemed to be paying them any attention.

"How didn't anyone hear that?" asked Sophie, "It was so loud." Before any of them could speak, a square door suddenly opened at the spot where Charlie had hit it.

"Hello everybody, Chester told me you would come knocking," said a strange little man inside the tree. He was about 75 centimetres tall; he had a funny little pointed hat which looked to be made of acorn cups. He had pointy ears and wore a brown waistcoat over a green shirt, red trousers and black boots.

"You look like an elf," said Charlie, plucking up courage to talk to the little man.

"That's because I am an elf, a tree elf," he replied.

"Are you real? Because we've only ever heard of elves in stories," said Sophie.

"Of course I am. I'm talking to you, aren't I?" said the elf.

Jack said, "That door wasn't there before, how did that happen?"

"It's a secret door of course. It has to be a secret or everyone would be coming in and we can't have that, can we?" asked the elf, smiling.

"Is this the start of the adventure?" asked Freddie.

"It certainly is, Freddie," said the elf.

Freddie gasped, "How do you know my name?"

"I know all the names of the Rainbow Gang; Chester told me all about you."

"You know Chester?" asked Billy.

"Yes I do, Billy, I've known him for a very long time."

"But when did he tell you about us? We only left him a little while ago," said Charlie.

"He often visits me to let me know all the latest news. I've known about you for a couple of days."

"So you were expecting us?" asked Robbie.

"Yes, I was watching out for you but I didn't know which tree you would choose."

"What's your name?" said Freddie.

"I wondered when you would ask that," the elf replied. "'Rooty', that's my name," said the elf, standing up straight and pushing his chest out proudly.

"Why are you called 'Rooty'?" asked Sophie.

"Because I spend most of my time down among the tree roots!"

"What, underground, you mean?" asked Billy.

"Yes, most of the time," said Rooty, "But we've got to get organised; when have you all got to be home?"

"We all normally have to go by 5 o'clock," said Jack, "and it's 4 o'clock now."

"OK, I'm going to demonstrate something to you. Charlie and Freddie are coming with me and the rest of you wait here;

we won't be long. Grab your bean lights and come in here," Rooty said, standing back to let the brothers in.

Chapter 8

Charlie and Freddie stepped inside the tree. There wasn't much room. Rooty pressed a wooden square on the wall. The door silently closed. It was very dark but only for a second or two. Suddenly, Rooty's hat lit up like an electric light. "Put your bean lights on," said Rooty.

"We don't have any beans," said Charlie.

"Ah, you should have brought the bean pouch. Never mind, I have some." He reached into his pocket and pulled out a couple of acorns. Freddie was struggling to get his bean light to fit. "Let me help you," said Rooty. He adjusted the straps and it fitted Freddie's head.

"Here, take a bean each and pop them into the cups and onto the spike. Don't forget to close the top or it might fall out." The boys did as Rooty said and the inside of the tree was suddenly quite bright. In the middle of the tree was what looked like a small square platform. It had rails on each side. "OK boys, step onto that square," said Rooty. The boys ducked under the rails and huddled together alongside their new friend. "Hold tight," said Rooty as he pressed a button on one of the rails.

The platform slowly started moving downwards. The boys gripped the rail. All they could see was earth and roots. The roots seemed to move as the shadows cast by the lights changed positions.

"Charlie," said Freddie, "I'm getting scared!"

"Don't worry, Freddie, I'm sure Rooty won't let anything happen," replied Charlie, although he was getting a little worried himself.

"You're completely safe," said Rooty.

"How far down are we going?" asked Freddie.

"We'll be there in a few more seconds!" said Rooty as the platform began to come to a stop. The boys looked around. It was a bit dark but they could see what looked like a tunnel. "Step out boys," said Rooty. They stepped into the tunnel, which went off in three directions—left, right and straight ahead. The tunnels were quite big. Charlie guessed they were about two metres high. There were what looked like lights at regular intervals along the tunnel walls.

"Are they more bean lights?" asked Charlie.

"No, these are different," said Rooty, taking a glass container off a hook on the side of the tunnel. "These are grub lights." The boys looked into the jars and there were several fat glowing grubs.

"What are they?" asked Freddie. The grubs were rolling around inside the jar. At first, they looked white but where they were touching each other, they gave off a yellowish glow. The more they wriggled, the yellower the light shone.

"They are the larva of the tunnel moths, and look there! Here come some." The brothers looked where Rooty pointed. Flying down the tunnel were three moths. They were quite big. Charlie reckoned they were as big as pigeons.

Freddie said, "They're as big as birds!"

"They are," said Rooty, "But watch this." He clapped his hands and immediately the moths glowed a beautiful blue colour.

"Wow," said the brothers at the same time.

"They'll shine like that for several minutes. Put your arm out, Charlie," said Rooty. Charlie held his arm out and the first moth to arrive settled on it.

Freddie said, "Can I do it?" and stuck his arm out. The second glowing moth landed on his arm. Rooty put his arm out and the third one fluttered onto his little arm. "They are very light," said Freddie.

"They are, aren't they? They are our friends. We call them silent lights," said Rooty. "If they are near us and we make a noise, they'll come to us."

"Where do the tunnels go?" said Charlie.

"They lead to other tunnels that are all connected. It's how we move around down here."

"You said we…how many of you live down here and are you all tree elves?" asked Charlie.

"There are many elves who live down here but they aren't all tree elves, some are digger elves. They obviously do the digging when we have to make new tunnels or repair damaged ones."

"Is that all of you?" said Freddie.

"No," said Rooty. "There's many more; some are senior elves. These elves make all the important decisions."

"Like what?" asked Charlie.

"They tell which trees need looking after most. Who works where, who looks after the moles and hogs."

"Moles and hogs?" said Freddie.

"Yes, we use moles for digging and hogs for transport," said Rooty.

"What do you mean by hogs—pigs?" said Charlie.

"No, hogs are what you call hedgehogs but a lot bigger. Come with me and I'll show you," said Rooty. Rooty moved off down the tunnel to the right. Charlie and Freddie followed.

"Wait a minute, Rooty, shouldn't we be going back up to the park? Don't forget, we've got to be home at 5 o'clock!" said Charlie.

"We've got plenty of time left, you'll see," Rooty said, smiling. Charlie and Freddie followed the elf down the tunnel. For someone with such short legs, he moved pretty fast. The boys were almost running to keep up. Ahead, they could see a bright light on one side of the tunnel. There was a large opening on the right. Rooty stopped and pointed inside. It was a large chamber and in it were what looked like large stables with several large hedgehogs.

Charlie gasped, "They're as big as horses!"

Freddie stood behind Charlie and asked, "Are they real?"

"Yes, very real; come and meet one," said Rooty, opening one of the stables. There it was—a giant hedgehog. It was wonderful. It was about one and a half metres high and two metres long with a shiny wet nose, big brown eyes and little round ears. Its body was dark brown and its spines were light brown with pale ends. Charlie and Freddie just stood and stared, looking at each other and back to the 'hog'. "Well,"

Rooty said, "What do you think?"

"It—it's amazing," said Charlie.

"It's massive," said Freddie.

"Excuse me," said the hedgehog, "I'm not that big!" Freddie staggered backwards and sat down on the floor. Charlie just opened his mouth but no words came out.

"Perhaps, I should have told you that not only are the hogs big but they can also speak," chuckled Rooty. There were other hedgehogs in the stables and they all chuckled together. "The hogs are all friendly and gentle; they won't harm you," said Rooty.

"What do they do down here?" asked Freddie.

"Well, if you look over there, you will see several small carts. Some are for transporting things and others are for riding in. We have special harnesses that fit round the hogs' chests. They are very strong and quite fast."

"Do they have names?" asked Freddie.

"Of course," said Rooty. He looked at the first hog and said, "Tell them your name."

"Hello boys, my name is Quill," said the first hog.

"Hello," said the boys.

"Quill is quite a common name among boy bighogs but I'm the only one in this stable block," said Quill.

"Hello," said the hog in the next stable. "My name is Rose."

"Hello," said the boys again.

"You're not very talkative, are you?" said Rose.

"Well, we've never met any animals that could talk," said Freddie.

"Animals? Animals?" said Rose, "We're not animals, we're bighogs."

"Sorry," said Freddie, "I didn't know."

"That's alright," said Quill, "We were quite shocked the first time we saw grounders."

"Is that what you call people from above?" asked Charlie.

"Yes," said Rooty, "Everybody down here are 'unders'."

"Grounders and Unders," said Charlie. "That's really clever." There were five other bighogs in the stable block; they all introduced themselves. Their names were Dolly, Max, Tiny (who was actually bigger than the rest), Chuck and Grub. They seemed really pleased to meet the boys.

"I can't wait to tell the others about all of this," said Freddie.

"Oh yes, the others," said Charlie, "We are going to be late going back home."

"OK, let's leave now," said Rooty, "Say goodbye to the boys."

"Bye," said all the bighogs.

"See you soon," said Freddie.

"Bye," said Charlie.

On the way back to the platform, Rooty, Charlie and Freddie were followed by several moths—silent lights. At the platform, the boys and Rooty climbed on board. "Hold on," said Rooty as he pressed another button on the handrail.

Chapter 9

"Did you see that?" said Robbie. "That door closed and you can't see where it was now!"

"And it didn't make any noise either!" said Jack.

"I wonder where Charlie and Freddie are going?" said Sophie.

"Yes; they better hadn't be too long. We've all got to be home by five," replied her brother.

As they spoke, the door opened again. "Did you forget something?" asked Billy as the boys peered out.

"What do you mean?" asked Charlie, stepping out.

"Well, you've only just gone."

"But we've been gone ages," said Charlie.

"Yeah, you won't believe what we've seen," added Freddie.

"No, you can't have been anywhere because as soon as the door closed, it opened up again," argued Robbie.

"Rooty, is this more magic?" asked Jack, looking at his watch. "Because my watch says it's only two minutes past four now."

"You're right, Jack, it is magic; time is different once you enter the tree roots."

"How long did you think you had been gone then?" asked Sophie.

"I suppose at least half an hour, maybe more," said Charlie.

"Really?" said Sophie, "Because it was as if the door closed and opened again almost straightaway."

"But we've been gone ages," said Freddie, "We've seen loads of stuff. Grub lights, moth lights, giant talking hedgehogs and big tunnels."

"What?" the others exclaimed together.

"Honestly, it's true," said Charlie.

"It is true," said Rooty, "and you'll all get the chance to see all that and more when you all go down together."

"Can we go now?" asked Billy.

"Not now because I'll have to make some arrangements before you go down. I'll leave you now so you can talk." Rooty stepped back into the old oak tree, the door silently closed and he was gone. The door suddenly opened again. "Come and knock again the day after tomorrow. Bye." The oak door closed again.

"Come on, Charlie and Freddie, tell us exactly what happened," said Robbie.

"Yes, every detail," said the twins together. Everyone laughed. For the next half hour, Charlie and Freddie told the others everything. They had to keep stopping when one of them would ask a question. When they finished telling them about their adventure, the others were quiet.

"I can't believe you did all that and were only gone for about a minute," said Robbie.

"It's weird—grubs, moths and giant hedgehogs. I can't wait," said Jack.

"It really was amazing down there. What I want to know is what we've got to do to help the unders," said Charlie.

"What if we have to help them look after the trees?
We know they need help 'cos they're all looking sad," said Sophie.

"That's right, but it's ginormous down there; we only saw three tunnels and they all disappeared into the distance," Charlie said.

"I wonder if there are any other keepers and chests?" said Freddie, sounding very grown-up.

"I hadn't thought of that," said Charlie. "Perhaps there are others. We'll have to ask Chester or Rooty."

"Yes, and we'll have to ask him about the moles. He said they use them for digging and there are digger elves too!" said Freddie.

"I wonder if they are giant moles?" said Billy.

"I suppose they must be if they dig the tunnels," Charlie said.

"I wonder what they all eat down there," Jack said thoughtfully.

"I don't know about the elves," said Charlie, "but I do know that hedgehogs eat worms and slugs and snails. I'm not sure about moles though; you'd think they'd eat worms 'cos they live underground most of the time."

"If the bighogs are as big as you said, they would have to have big worms to eat, wouldn't they?" said Sophie.

"They'd be massive if they're on the same scale," said Jack.

"How big would that be?" asked Freddie.

"I dunno," said Jack, "perhaps half a metre long."

"I don't think I'd like that," said Sophie.

"I don't think any of us would," said Robbie.

"Or snails and slugs," said Billy.

"Definitely not," said Charlie.

"More questions for Chester," said Billy and Sophie together.

"Stop it!" said Freddie, "You're doing it again!"

"Sorry, we don't do it on purpose; it just happens," said Billy. "We'd better get going soon or we'll be late home."

"OK, we'll meet at the back of Charlie and Freddie's garden tomorrow after school," said Robbie. They all agreed.

When Charlie and Freddie went home from the twins' house, their mum was just preparing their dinner. "What's for dinner, Mum? We're starving," said Freddie.

"Chicken, chips and peas," said Mrs White, "What have you been up to that you are so hungry?"

"Oh, just the usual—in the park on our bikes and messing about with the others."

"Yeah, it's been really interesting," said Freddie. Charlie glared at Freddie. "What's so interesting then? You go to the park most days after school."

"Well, we were looking at the big trees and they seem to be suffering more than the others. Emma told us Dave was at a meeting today and might have some news."

"Since when did you start calling Billy and Sophie's mum and dad, Emma and Dave?" asked their mum.

"Earlier today, they said they'd like us to use their names. It feels a bit funny," admitted Charlie.

"They want us to call them Emma and Dave; they said it makes them feel young," said Freddie.

"I suppose Billy and Sophie will want to call me and Dad, Carol and Mike."

"I don't think so; they think it's weird but funny," said Charlie.

"I think we'll stick with Mr and Mrs White for now, don't you?" said Mrs White. "Aw Mum, it'd be cool if they did!" said Freddie.

"Come on, sit at the table, dinner's ready," said their mum.

After dinner, the boys decided they wanted to talk to Chester. So while their parents ate their dinner, they asked whether it was OK if they went to the shed to clean and oil their bikes.

"Of course," said Dad, "Use the blue oilcan but don't get the oil on the brake blocks or the wheel rims."

"OK," said the boys together. "Oh no," said Freddie, "We're turning into Billy and Sophie." The boys left the kitchen, laughing all the way to the shed.

They unlocked the shed and went inside. There was no sign of Chester. The tins and boxes and rags were just that— tins and boxes and rags. Charlie and Freddie moved their bikes outside, went back into the shed and had a good look round but there was definitely no Chester.

"What's happened?" said Freddie, "Why's he not here?"

"I don't know, Freddie, perhaps he's busy somewhere else. Perhaps he's talking to another keeper. Come on, we'd better get on and clean and oil our bikes or Mum and Dad will get suspicious."

"What if he doesn't come back?" said Freddie, looking upset. "Our adventure has only just started."

"We know we can contact Rooty and he speaks to Chester. I'm sure it's going to be alright."

"Freddie," said Charlie, looking very serious. "What happened to the old leather backpack? I didn't pick it up. Did you see it?"

"Oh no," said Freddie, "We can't have lost it."

"Perhaps one of the others picked it up," said Charlie, "I think we should go and look in the park if Mum and Dad will let us."

"We could say that we are just going to see what our bikes are like now that we've oiled them," Freddie suggested.

"Good idea, Freddie, let's go."

The boys rushed into the kitchen.

"Mum, Dad! Can we take our bikes into the park just to see what they're like?" said Freddie.

"What do you mean, Freddie?" said Dad.

"Now that we've oiled them, to see if they're better than before," said Charlie.

"OK then, just for five minutes and leave the gate hooked back so that we can see you."

The boys dashed over to the far side of the park and checked around the trees but there was no sign of the old leather backpack. "What shall we do, Charlie?" asked Freddie, "Suppose someone else has found it?"

"I hope not, but if they did, what would they find? All the special stuff or the things that Danny and Jake saw, you know…the snacks and all that."

"Did we put the bean lights in there? I can't remember."

"Yes, we did. Woody was in there too."

"Where can it be?" said Freddie.

Charlie and Freddie were just getting back on their bikes when they suddenly saw Billy racing towards them. He skidded to a stop. "What's up, Billy?" asked Charlie.

"Look what I've got!" said Billy, whipping off the backpack.

"Where was it?" asked Charlie.

"You know how tidy Sophie is. She picked it up and put it on as we were leaving and when we got home, she went upstairs and put it in her bedroom. It wasn't until after we'd had our dinner that she remembered. I got it out and went to your house and your dad said you were testing your bikes and so I came straight over."

"Well done, Billy, we were really worried. We thought we'd lost it."

Chapter 10

Everybody met up in the park as agreed. Charlie and Freddie had earlier told them about Chester not being in their shed and how they thought they had lost the backpack.

They all decided that they should check whether Chester the chest was back in the shed. To everyone's relief, Chester was there in the middle of the floor. His lid was off and when they looked in, they could see four new bean lights. Billy, Sophie, Jack and Robbie got really excited. There was also another folded piece of paper. Charlie lifted it out and unfolded it. The note read:

"Sorry, I've been away, I've been a bit busy. I can't talk to you today; that's why I left this note.

I've been visiting other keepers. The problem that's affecting the trees is more serious than we thought. We believe we know what's causing it, though. Go and visit Rooty again; all of you will travel this time. He'll let you know what to do.

Bye for now, Chester."

The gang all started talking at once. "Stop!" shouted Jack, taking charge.

"Yes, come on, one at a time," said Charlie.

"OK, me first," said Sophie. "Does this mean that we'll all be going underground?"

"Well, it sounds like it. We'll have to see what Rooty says."

"Look," said Freddie, pointing at the corner of the shed. "It's the backpack."

Sure enough, the backpack was there.

"But I left it upstairs under the bed," said Charlie.

"More magic," said Billy.

"Well, I think that we should put our bean lights in it with the others," said Robbie. Robbie opened the backpack and put the new bean lights inside. "There's two more pouches in here," he said. He took them out, untied them and tipped out the contents. "More beans, quite a lot more."

"How long do they last?" asked Sophie.

"I don't really know," said Charlie, "But they were still on when we got back from going down with Rooty and we were down there for quite a while."

"The lights went out when Rooty opened the door at the time we got back," said Freddie.

"You're right," said Charlie, "I remember now."

"Do you think we should all take some?" Jack asked.

Robbie counted the beans—there were 10 in one bag and 11 in the second.

"There must be some in the other pouch; we didn't take them out before," said Charlie.

Robbie rummaged in the bottom of the backpack. "You're right," he said, tipping out more beans from the original pouch, "There are six."

"So that's 27 altogether; if we take four each, that's 24 and that will leave three spare," said Billy.

Robbie counted out the beans and gave them to the others. They all put them in their pockets. "That leaves seven, my four and three for emergencies. Shall I look after the extra ones?" The others all agreed.

"Shall we go to the park and knock for Rooty?" said Freddie.

The six Rainbow Gang members collected their bikes and set off to the far side of the park. When they arrived at the big old oak tree, there were several adults nearby. Some were walking dogs, others were jogging and some were with their children just having a good time.

The gang parked their bikes against the fence that separated the park from the woods. "We'll have to wait until it's a bit more quiet," said Charlie.

"I can't wait to go underground," said Sophie.

"I think we all feel the same," said Jack.

After a few minutes, the other park users moved away from the big oak's vicinity.

"I've just had a thought," said Robbie. "What are we going to do with our bikes when we go into the tree? We can't leave them here; it would look a bit funny, six bikes all leaning against the fence and no one here. I haven't got my lock with me so anyone could steal it."

"I've got mine," said Jack.

"Me too," said Billy, "but we can't lock all six with just two padlocks and anyway, it would look odd."

"But if we go in and come out as quick as Charlie and Freddie did, they would only be here without us for a minute," said Robbie.

"That's true," said Charlie, "but supposing someone comes by just as we come back?"

"We'll have to speak to Rooty," decided Charlie.

"No one's around now; shall we knock on the tree?" said Freddie.

Charlie took off the backpack and took out Woody. "OK, let's do it," he said.

As before, the noise of the mallet hitting the old oak was really loud but again, nobody else seemed to hear it. The door opened and there stood Rooty.

"Hello everyone," said Rooty, "This is my friend, Conker."

Another elf leaned out from behind Rooty and smiled. "Hello," he said.

He was almost exactly the same as Rooty, except he did not have red trousers, his were blue.

"Hello," the gang replied together.

"OK," said Rooty, "Let's get moving."

"Before we go, Rooty, we don't know what to do about our bikes. It might look a bit funny if our bikes are here and we're not," said Charlie.

"Good point," said Conker, "But I can take care of that." He reached into his waistcoat and took out a small blue bag. He threw it towards the bikes and it landed among the bikes and burst, showering the bikes in a blue mist. When the mist cleared, the bikes were nowhere to be seen.

"How did you do that?" asked Billy and Sophie.

"It's magic," said Conker, smiling. "Don't worry; they will be safe until we come back. Come on; because of the size of the up-and-down platform, we can only take three of you at a time."

"Is that what you call it?" asked Freddie.

"Yes, an up-and-down platform," replied Rooty. "Why?"

"We call things like that 'lifts'," said Jack.

"But our platforms don't only lift, they lower as well," said Rooty.

"That's a fair comment," said Jack, looking a bit puzzled.

"That's very logical," said Charlie.

"Is it?" said Rooty, "Anyway, let's get moving. Charlie, Freddie and Sophie, you'll be first.

Conker will go down with you and send the up-and-down back for us. You boys wait here; I'll close the door and open it as soon as the up-and-down returns," said Rooty.

Charlie, Freddie and Sophie stepped through the door, put on their bean lights, climbed onto the platform and descended to the bottom. Rooty stayed inside the tree waiting. As soon as the platform returned, he opened the door and the rest of the gang stepped inside, put on their bean lights and got onto the platform with Rooty.

"Here we go," said Jack.

"Hold on boys," said Rooty, "This is where it starts." He pressed the button on the rail and the platform slowly went down.

Jack, Billy and Robbie looked excited in the glow of their bean lights and Rooty's hat.

Chapter 11

Sophie and the brothers stood quietly with Conker.

They could hear the platform coming down.

"It won't be long," said Conker.

Sophie was looking around at the three tunnels and wondering where they led. "Which one goes to the hog stables?" she asked.

"Down there," Charlie pointed to the right.

"I can't wait to meet the big hogs," Sophie said.

"There is lots to see and lots of elves and others to meet," said Conker.

"Ah, here are your friends." The platform came to a halt and Rooty and the others got off.

"OK everyone, follow me," said Rooty as he set off down the left-hand tunnel. He was travelling at his usual speed.

"Where are we going?" asked Sophie, "I wanted to meet the hogs."

"You will, all in good time," said Rooty over his shoulder.

"He's quick for such a little fellow," said Robbie.

"Yes," said Charlie, "Have you noticed the grub lights?"

"Yes, they're really neat," said Jack.

Up ahead, they could see a large pool of light. There was a large opening on the left side of the tunnel. It looked like Rooty was heading that way. He stopped in the light. "Hurry up, you lot," he said and pointed into the large opening.

Everyone filed into what was a very large chamber. It was very, very large and there were lots of elves in there.

"Wow," said Robbie, "look at all these elves."

They all stopped what they were doing and looked at the strangers who had just entered.

"Pay attention, everybody," shouted Rooty. "These are our latest grounders come to help us and this one here," he said, pointing at Charlie, "he is a keeper."

All the elves jumped to their little booted feet and started clapping. The group of friends all felt a bit embarrassed but also excited.

"This chamber is our meeting place… We eat here and make plans here. And over there," he pointed to the far side, "that's where the senior elves make all the big decisions. You'll meet them soon. Now, have you noticed that we don't all dress the same?" asked Rooty.

"Yes," said Freddie, "Conker's got blue trousers."

"Well done, Freddie," said Rooty, "That's because he's a driver—he looks after the hogs and moles."

"So all the different-coloured trousers mean that elves have different jobs?"

"Are there any lady elves?" asked Sophie.

"Yes, of course. Look around; there are many out here."

When the gang looked, they could see that there were lady elves in the chamber. They looked like Rooty but had yellow hair and dresses with aprons. The aprons were of different colours. The gang assumed that this meant they had different jobs. They also had black boots; in fact, everyone was wearing boots—black, shiny boots.

"There are lots of jobs down here," said Rooty. "Woodworkers, diggers, gardeners, moth keepers, cooks, weavers and many more."

"Where do you all live?" asked Sophie.

"We all have homes, of course," said Rooty, "I'll show you some later."

"How long will we be here with you?" asked Charlie.

"We don't know," replied Rooty. "It depends on how long the jobs take but don't worry, I showed you how time is different down here so your parents won't miss you."

"What do you eat?" asked Freddie, "And what do the hogs and moles eat?"

"We only eat fruits and vegetables and nuts. We don't eat meat. We do eat eggs. We have special hens down here. The

56

elves who tend to the hens are called 'eggers'," said Conker. "They wear green trousers."

"What about the hogs and moles? What do they eat?"

"Well, the hogs eat lots of things: insects, frogs, eggs and berries and also fruit. The moles eat mainly worms and nuts," said a new elf.

"Oh hello," said Rooty to the newcomer. "This is Huff, he's a hogsman and he takes care of the hogs and moles."

"Hello, pleased to meet you."

"Hello," said the gang.

"Look," said Freddie, "he's got yellow trousers."

"Do all the different jobs have different-coloured trousers?" asked Charlie.

"Yes or different-coloured shirts," said Rooty.

"How do you remember all the colours?" said Sophie.

"We grow up with them so eventually, we get to know them all," replied Rooty.

"Are there children elves?" asked Jack. "I haven't seen any."

"Of course, there are; we don't come from eggs. All the children are at school."

"You've got schools?" said Freddie.

"Yes, how do you think we learn?" said Rooty.

"So you have teacher elves?" asked Robbie, "What colour trousers do they wear?"

"The male teachers wear white shirts, black waistcoats, black trousers and boots. The lady teachers wear white dresses with black aprons and boots," said Rooty.

"But don't worry; you don't need to know who does what and what colours they wear. Just be sure to remember that we are your friends and will all help you in your adventures."

"That's a relief," said Jack.

"Anyway, come on, I'll show you to your quarters," said Rooty. "Follow me."

As the gang filed out of the main door, all the elves said either, "Bye", "See you soon" or "See you later."

Rooty led them further down the tunnel until he came to a wooden door a short distance from the main room. There was a big grub light above the door and a wooden sign read, 'Keepers'.

Rooty pushed open the door. The room was very light; there were lots of grub lights. In the middle of the room was a long bench with stools all around it. There were beds around the outside against the walls. There were twelve beds in total. Three small sofas were spread around. There were two doors at the back of the room; each had a sign on it—one saying 'girls' and the other one saying 'boys'.

"These are the shower rooms and toilets," said Rooty. When the gang looked more closely, each bed had a large fluffy white towel on it and what looked like a folded shirt.

"What's this?" asked Freddie, picking up a 'shirt'.

"We know you wear pyjamas at home but we only have nightshirts," said Rooty.

"I'm not wearing a nightshirt," said Freddie.

"Nor me," said the other boys at the same time.

"Well, I will," said Sophie, "Don't be so rude; the elves are giving us somewhere to sleep and something to wear in bed."

"We'll look funny," said Charlie.

"Yes, you might think so but you'll be very warm. It can be a bit chilly down here at night. Anyway, you'll need to take your clothes off so that the washers can clean them. There are hatches over there," he said, pointing to two small doors next to the bathrooms. "Put your clothes in there and they will be back in the morning—clean."

"Are there going to be other children here with us?" asked Sophie. "I've counted and there are twelve beds."

"Chester has told me that there may be another keeper and her friends coming but not yet," said Rooty.

"A girl keeper?" said Sophie excitedly.

"Yes, Chester will let me know. Right, who's hungry?"

"I expect we all are," said Charlie, "But when are you going to tell us about what we are going to do?"

"OK, let's have dinner first and then I'll take you to meet the elder elves and they will explain."

The gang had not noticed that there were two more doors in the walls. As they walked to the bench, these doors opened and several lady elves dressed all in white came in carrying plates of food. Plates of eggs—boiled and scrambled, plates of strange little breads, apples, berries and nuts. There was a large bowl of soup that smelt delicious. Behind the lady elves was a small boy elf carrying a tray full of drinks.

"Sit down and enjoy your dinner," said Rooty, "Do you mind if I join you?"

Chapter 12

The gang was a bit unsure about the food but after a few minutes, they were tucking in. The food, they decided, was wonderful. They had never tasted anything like it.

As they ate their dinner, they asked Rooty lots of questions. How many elves are there? Did they live all around the world? Did they ever live above ground? Is there a king or queen elf? Do they have soldiers?

Rooty replied, "Yes, elves do live all around the world. Some elves do still live above ground but most of us live underground. Many, many years ago, we all lived in your world. It was a different time then and there were many different types of people living above ground."

"We shared the world with each other and lived in peace; it was like that for a very long time—a very, very long time. Mankind was becoming cleverer and built big villages with lots of homes and farms. Some of the other land dwellers were becoming jealous. Especially the Big'uns, what you call 'giants'."

"Giants!" said the gang almost at the same time.

"You mean, there used to be giants living here?" asked Charlie.

"They still live here but not above ground, not even down here. They live in a world below us," Rooty said, pointing to the floor.

"Why don't they come out?" asked Freddie.

"It was agreed between all the people on Earth that there wasn't room for all of us to live together peacefully. That was after there had been a big war between two big groups, mankind and us elves with the snow people and the sea dwellers fought against the big'uns, the trolls and the troggs.

I wasn't alive then but our history tells us that it was a very bad time. After the war, the trolls went back to live in the mountains and the troggs just disappeared, never to be seen or heard of again. The big'uns found their way below us and discovered a world where they could live without ever having to come back to the surface again."

"You mean, they still live below where we are standing?" asked Robbie.

"Yes, but just recently, there has been a problem with the flow of water. It's not getting to where it normally goes. It's somehow being diverted to where the big'uns are. We've heard some activity and we can hear noises but we don't know what the noises are, but the big'uns seem to be taking the water from the water rocks that we, the elves and you grounders, need to survive. For some reason, the big'uns are draining water down to bigworld. They've always had their own water supply but they are using ours and we've got to stop them."

"Is that why the trees in our world are looking sad?" asked Sophie.

"Exactly," said Rooty, "And as I'm a tree elf, with my companions, we have to find a way to stop the big'uns."

"And that's why you've contacted us to help?" asked Jack.

"What can we do to help?" said Charlie, "Can't Chester use his magic to stop it?"

"Unfortunately, magic doesn't work underground," said Rooty, "It never has. If it did, we wouldn't need our grounder friends to help."

"But what can we do against giants? We're only kids," said Freddie.

"That's right, but you 'kids', as you put it, are bigger than us elves—well, most of us anyway."

"You mean, there are bigger elves? How big are they?" asked Charlie.

"Well, some are as big as Jack, but there are more that are the same size as the rest of you. They're bigger than any of us regular elves anyway."

"Well, what are we going to do?" asked Billy and Sophie together. Freddie laughed. "OK Freddie, we know," said Sophie.

"Sorry," said Freddie.

"Look," said Rooty, "Tomorrow I'll take you to meet the elders who will explain everything and hopefully have a plan."

At that moment, the door from the tunnel opened and in walked another tree elf. "Hello Rooty," he said.

"Hi Rock," said Rooty.

"I've got something to show you; come in everyone." He stood to one side and in walked four girls, grounder girls. "This is Maggie. Maggie is a keeper and these are her friends. They've come to help," said Rock.

"Welcome," said Rooty, "Come and meet the others."

The four girls walked forward and Rock and Rooty introduced them all to each other. Apart from Maggie, who had red hair, the other three all had fair hair. Their names were Emma, Lauren and Sam.

"Are you hungry, girls?" Rooty asked.

"Yes, we are," said Maggie.

"OK," Rooty said, "I'll organise some food for you; while I'm gone, you can all get to know each other."

To start with, things were a bit awkward but after a few minutes, the children were chatting away easily. The Rainbow Gang immediately realised that Lauren and Sam were twins, identical twins.

"What's the chance of two keepers both having twins as best friends?" said Robbie.

"It's amazing," said Freddie, "I suppose you say the same things at the same time?"

"Yes, we do," said the new twins together. Everybody burst out laughing. Freddie laughed the longest.

The doors, the gang realised, were from the kitchen and once again, the lady elves came in bringing food for Maggie and her friends.

The ten 'grounders' sat eating and talking. It became apparent that the girls lived in a small town about five miles from the Rainbow Gang's town. Both towns' football teams play in the same league and are archrivals. Charlie spent a long time talking to Maggie asking about how she was a keeper like him. She has a chest as well and knows Chester.

"Has Rock told you about the giants?" Charlie asked Maggie.

"Yes, he told us on the way here; we travelled in a sort of cart pulled by a giant hedgehog."

"We've met some bighogs; do you know that they can speak?"

"Yes, our one was very chatty all the way here; her name is Sky and she's very fast," Maggie said, pulling a face.

"Has Rock said what we're going to have to do exactly?"

"No," Maggie replied. "He said we'll find out when we meet the elders tomorrow."

"I really can't think of anything we could do that the elves can't, apart from the fact that we're bigger than most of them," said Charlie. "I don't get it."

"I know what you mean," said Maggie. "From what Rock said, it's all to do with water, which the giants are taking."

"Yes, Rooty told us the same; he said there's never been a problem before."

"Come on, you two," said Jack, "What are you talking about?"

"Are you 'special' friends?" teased Freddie.

"Don't be silly, Fred," said Maggie.

"Oh no," said Sophie, "Don't call him that, not Fred, only Freddie, 'cos he gets all sulky."

"No, I don't!" shouted Freddie.

"Alright, Freddie, Maggie didn't know," said Charlie, "and Sophie's only having a bit of fun."

"Well, alright then, but remember, it's Freddie!"

Maggie asked why they were known as the Rainbow Gang. Charlie explained and Maggie asked if she could be an honorary member as she had red hair and it was decided that as the girls were known only as 'The Girls' at home, they could all be honorary members.

"Sophie, in that case, you can be an honorary member of 'The Girls'," said Emma.

"Thanks," said Sophie, "That's nice."

"We still don't know what we're here for," said Jack, "Has anyone got any idea?" The room became silent as the group all looked at each other.

"That's a no then!" said Charlie, "I guess we'll have to wait until we meet the elders in the morning."

Rooty and Rock had been standing in the corner talking. "I think it would be a good idea if you thought about getting some sleep; it will probably be a busy day tomorrow."

"Can't you tell us anything more about what we've got to do?" asked Robbie.

"Unfortunately not. It's not up to us; the elders will tell you," said Rock.

"When you get undressed, if you've got anything in your pockets, put it on the bedside table in the small dishes. It will be safe there," said Rooty.

The girls grabbed their towels and nightshirts and went into their shower room. The boys all changed in the main room; they gathered up their clothes and put them in the washing hatch. They stood looking at each other and then the girls appeared. There was much laughing.

"Well, I don't know about the rest of you but I'm tired," said Sophie. The others all agreed.

"Let's go to bed then," said Jack. The boys went to one side, the girls to the other. One of the kitchen doors opened and a lady elf came in and tidied all the plates away and cleaned the bench. Another lady elf started taking the grub lights away but left two behind so that the room was not completely dark.

The children all settled down. "Goodnight, everyone," said Charlie.

"Goodnight," they all replied.

Within ten minutes, they were all sound asleep.

Chapter 13

The children all woke up at about the same time. They decided that it was the smell of the food that was being brought in by the lady elves. They were disappointed when they realised it was porridge. But it smelt so good that they could not resist and just like last night's dinner, it was delicious. There was also toasted bread and jam. They ate all that they were given.

Rooty entered the room.

"This food is lovely," said Sophie.

"Thank you," said Rooty, "I'll pass on your thanks to the lady elves—they will like that. Now, if you'd all like to get washed and dressed, Rock and I will take you to the main hall to meet the elders."

After 15 minutes, all the children were washed or showered and dressed in their freshly washed clothes.

"Right then," said Rock as he appeared at the door, "Follow us."

The Rainbow Gang and The Girls hurried to keep up with Rock and Rooty, whose little legs carried them quickly to the main room.

Inside, it was full with many elves. At the front stood a group of older-looking elves, both men and women. The elf at the front of the group clapped his hands and the room became very quiet.

"Here," he said in a loud voice, "are Charlie, Maggie and their friends, grounders, to help us." The gathered elves all started clapping and cheering.

The elf at the front let the cheering go on for a little while, then he held up his hands. Quickly, the room became quiet again. Addressing the children, he said, "Follow us please."

The elves moved back to let the elders and children move towards the far side of the room where two wooden doors opened to let them through. The doors were opened by two big elves who let the two groups through, closed the doors and waited outside. There were lots of seats.

"Please sit down and make yourselves comfortable."

Two of the lady elves from the kitchen passed round glasses of juice.

"Let me introduce myself, I'm not actually an elder. I'm the King, King Bigfists. If you look at my hands, you'll realise why."

The children all looked at the King's hands and they were big, very big. "And this beautiful elf is my queen, Queen Blush!"

The queen was a very tall, slim lady elf; she was very pretty. She was dressed completely in pale blue and she smiled a big smile at the children.

"Now these other elves are the elders and they will now tell you about our and your problems," said the King.

Another elf stepped forward; he was as small as Rooty and Rock. "Good morning to you; my name is Larch." He bowed to the children. "Now we have a big problem and it's all because of the big'uns, one big'un in particular. His name is BigBum and he does indeed have a big bum. He is the son of the King of the big'uns, Ralph the Massive and Queen Very Loud."

The children were all giggling when they heard the giants' names.

"All big'uns have names that describe the way they look or behave; King Ralph is one of the biggest big'uns you'll ever see and his queen is the loudest lady big'un. Their son, BigBum, is always getting into trouble. Mostly, what he gets up to doesn't normally affect us unders or you grounders but this time, it does. We don't know how he actually managed it but he's got his bum stuck in a major waterway."

At this, the children all burst out laughing. Larch held up his hands. "Yes, it does sound funny but it's actually very serious."

The children went quiet.

"The waterway that is blocked by Big, er, King Ralph's son is a main route from a giant underground lake to all the aquifers in a vast area that makes its way up to your aboveground water."

"Is that why the trees where we live are looking a bit brown, even though it's not autumn yet?" asked Charlie.

"Exactly," said Larch, "What we think happened is that a certain big'un went swimming in the giant lake and somehow managed to get his, er, bottom stuck in the outlet to the waterway. At the moment, the water isn't high enough to harm Bigbum but eventually, he could drown! Although we don't get on with big'uns, we wouldn't want that to happen to him. The big'uns can't get to him because we think the route he took to get to the lake is now flooded."

"So how can we help; do you have a plan?" asked Jack.

"We think we have but it will be you children who have to put it into action. Anyone told you that elves don't swim and are a bit nervous around lakes and waterways?"

"We didn't know that," said Maggie, "Does it make a difference?"

"Well, it means that we can't help you as much as we'd like to. The plan is that you children will go to the lake, attach ropes to BigBum and, using hogs and moles, we'll try to pull him out."

"Do you think BigBum will let us tie ropes to him?" asked Robbie.

"And how will we get to him on the lake?" said Lauren and Sam at the same time. Freddie started laughing.

"Come on, Freddie," said Charlie, "This is serious stuff."

"We've built some boats!" said another one of the elders, looking really pleased with himself.

"But if you don't go near water, how do you know how to build boats?"

Rooty stood up. "Chester told us how to do it."

"You've spoken to Chester?" asked Sophie, "When?"

"Yesterday morning, he sent us pictures and instructions. A team of builder elves spent all day yesterday and most of the night making three boats. They are very pleased with the results," Rooty replied.

"Have they been tested?" asked Billy.

"Yes, are they watertight?" said Emma.

"What's watertight?" asked a lady elder elf.

"If you put a boat into water, it can't have any leaks or it will sink. Did Chester say anything about putting any stuff on the outside of the boats?"

"Yes," said Rock, "Chester told us to make a mixture of tree sap and crushed acorns boiled together and painted on the outside of the boats. We thought it was to make the boats look nice and shiny."

"But they haven't been tested on water?" asked Jack.

"Well, no," said Larch, "We thought you could do that when you get to the lake."

"But what happens if they leak? We won't be able to rescue BigBum," said Charlie.

"Well, we've done exactly as instructed by Chester and he always knows the right thing to do," said Rooty.

"How do we get to the lake?" asked Freddie.

A taller-than-average elf stood up; he was dressed in what looked like overalls. "My name is Norris," said the elf, "I'm the elder who looks after the digger elves. My digger elves have been very busy. They've built a tunnel that goes to the lake and I must say that they've done a magnificent job. It's big enough to accommodate all of you in two boats."

Rooty stood up again. "OK children, the plan is that you will slide down the tunnel to the water by ropes attached to the boats."

"Will we be able to see where we are going; will our bean lights make enough light to see across a lake?" asked Maggie.

"You'll be surprised how much light there will be. The water will glow pale blue as it reacts to the bean lights. Have you all got your bean lights with you and have you got your compasses?"

Charlie said, "I've got all of our lights and the compass in the backpack; what about you, Maggie?"

"Yes, we've got ours in a backpack as well, its back in the bedroom."

"Ours is back there as well," said Charlie.

"Good," said Rooty, "When you go down to the lake, we'll send some silent lights with you. When you eventually get to the water, you should be able to see BigBum off to the west. You'll see that the ropes have a big loop on the end. What you will have to do is persuade BigBum to put the loops around his wrists and hold onto the ropes; when he's done that, you'll signal to us."

"What will the signal be?" interrupted Freddie.

"We haven't decided yet," said Rooty.

"What about a whistle?" suggested Jack.

"What's a whistle?" asked Rooty.

"This is," said Jack, putting his fingers into his mouth and letting out a loud, shrill blast. All of the elves clamped their hands to their ears.

Rooty was the first to uncover his ears. "Goodness me," he said, "How did you do that?

It was so loud, can you all do that?"

"I can," said Charlie.

"Me too," said Robbie.

"And me," said Freddie.

"And me," said Maggie and Emma together.

Both sets of twins said that they had not learnt how to do it. "It's easy," said Freddie, "I'll show you."

"Not now, Freddie," said Charlie.

"I think that will work perfectly as a signal," said Rooty.

All of the other elves murmured in agreement.

"What happens if BigBum doesn't do what we tell him?" asked Sam.

"Explain to him that the water will eventually cover his head. I think he'll let you do it then," said Rooty.

"So when we've got the ropes on his wrists and Jack gives the signal, what next?" asked Charlie.

"The other ends of the ropes will be attached to a team of our biggest hogs and moles and we'll pull him out," said Rooty.

"Where will he go then; is there a way out for him?"

"When the water flows out through the waterway, the hole he came through will eventually be revealed and he can go back down where he belongs."

"But what about us in the boats?" asked Maggie, "Won't we go down the waterway hole?"

"Ah," said Rooty, "We hadn't thought about that."

"Well, I think you'd better think about it now," said Robbie, "Because none of us want to be sucked down a pipe full of water."

"No, of course not," said Rooty.

"If we manage to free BigBum, the ropes could be used to pull us back up the tunnel," said Emma.

"Of course," said Robbie, "Why wouldn't that work?"

"I can't see why not," said Charlie.

"Yeah, it's simple really," said Jack.

"I don't know why we didn't think of that," said Rooty.

"OK, that's a plan then," said Charlie.

"Yes indeed," said Larch, "I suggest all those involved meet at the tunnel top in about one hour."

"OK children, let's go back to the dormitory," said Rooty.

"What's a dormitory?" asked Freddie.

"It's where we slept last night," said Charlie, "Come on, let's go."

Maggie turned to Charlie. "Charlie," she said, "I'm a bit scared."

"I think we all are, but it's going to be a real adventure."

Chapter 14

When the children were ready, Rooty and Rock took them to one of the stables. Inside, there were two bighogs with a cart harnessed to each of them. In the front of the first one was Conker the driver, in the second was another driver elf who introduced himself as Chip.

Rooty divided the children into two groups: Maggie, Emma, Charlie, Freddie and Robbie were to travel with Conker. Lauren, Sam, Billy, Sophie and Jack were to travel with Chip.

They all clambered into the carts and sat down on seats that were quite comfortable. Conker called back from his seat at the front of the cart: "Our bighog today is Quill."

"Hello everyone," said Quill.

"Hello," the children replied.

"Freddie and I have met you before," said Charlie.

"I remember," said Quill, "Nice to see you again."

Chip introduced his bighog to the others. "This is Tiny," he said.

"Hello Tiny," replied his passengers.

"Why are you called Tiny?" asked Emma, "You look quite big to me."

"When I was young, I was little but I just kept growing."

"Right everybody, hold on, we're setting off," said Conker.

"What about Rooty and Rock?" called Freddie.

"They are coming with the rest of the hogs and the moles," replied Conker.

"OK hogs," said Chip, "Let's go."

The two groups left the stable and set off slowly down the tunnel. After a short while, the speed increased. The children held on tighter.

The tunnel turned to the right and started to go up. All along the tunnels, the grub lights came on and a large group of silent lights followed behind.

After about 15 minutes, they arrived at a large chamber that looked as if it was newly made. There were quite a lot of elves waiting. Lots of them were dressed like Norris—in overalls. Over to one side was a tunnel that appeared to go downwards. There was a rope tied across the entrance and on it, hung a sign:

'DANGER—WATER'.

The children saw the sign and all started whispering.

Conker could see what was going on; he stood up in the front of the cart. "The sign is to warn elves," he said, "So don't be alarmed."

Just then, the team of bighogs and moles arrived. The last mole to arrive was pulling a cart with the three boats on it.

Charlie turned to Robbie, "Why do you think they've built three boats if we'll be travelling in only two?"

"I've been wondering about that too," replied Robbie. "Let's ask Rooty."

They both jumped from the cart and went over to Rooty. "Rooty," called Charlie.

"Yes boys, how can I help?"

"Why are there three boats if we only need two?" asked Charlie.

"Two of our bravest elves are going to escort you."

"I thought elves were scared of water," said Robbie.

"As I said, these two elves are very brave."

"Why do we need an escort?" asked Charlie, "I thought we wouldn't be in danger?"

"You won't be in danger. It's just that some of the diggers thought they might have seen some clunkers."

"What are clunkers?" asked Maggie, who had just joined the boys.

"Clunkers are fish, big fish," said Rooty.

"Are they dangerous?" asked Maggie.

"How big are they?" asked Charlie.

"Do they bite?" asked Robbie.

"They don't bite, no, they definitely don't bite. They are about three metres long with very hard heads but they aren't dangerous unless they bash your boats," said Rooty.

"What do you mean…bash our boats? That's dangerous, isn't it? You're not telling us everything, Rooty, are you?" Jack said as he walked up.

"OK, clunkers shouldn't be in the lake; they belong in the land of the big'uns."

"How did they get in the lake?" asked Charlie.

"We are only guessing so we're not sure but they must have come up the tunnel that BigBum used. They have got very developed and muscular fins. They can walk and breathe on dry land. I know that sounds odd but it's a different world where the big'uns live," said Rooty.

"So could that have been the noises you heard?" asked Jack, "The clunkers walking up the tunnel?"

"Yes, we think so."

"How many clunkers are in the lake or don't you know?" said Charlie.

"We don't know but we know they won't harm you. If you haven't paid, they might tip you into the water," said Rooty.

"What do you mean…paid?" Both sets of twins said at the same time. No one laughed this time.

"Where big'uns live, there are lots of rivers and lots of ferries. The ferrymen giants use clunkers to get the money from anyone who hasn't paid and tries to get across the river. They bash the boat until those trying to sneak across pay up."

"You'll think I'm joking but I'm not. The clunkers have slots in their hard heads where you can put money."

"It sounds like a joke to me," said Freddie.

"What, you mean clunkers are like big money boxes?" said Billy.

"I don't know what a money box is but I guess its somewhere you keep money.

If that's right, yes, clunkers are like money boxes."

"How do the big'un ferrymen get the money out? Do they pick them up and shake them?" asked Freddie.

"That's what our spies tell us," said Rock.

"You have spies?" said Freddie.

"Of course, we have to keep an eye on the big'uns," replied Rooty.

"How do your spies get to—what do you call the world where the big'uns live?" asked Charlie.

"Big-land...Down-below...even under...under... There are lots of names," said Rooty.

"So how do your spies get there?"

"They use elf-sized tunnels, but they are secret."

"Are the spies down there now?" asked Charlie.

"Yes."

"What have they found out about BigBum being stuck; do the giants know he's missing?"

"Yes, they know he's missing but they don't know where he is."

"How long has he been stuck there?" asked Emma.

"We're not sure but we think eight days or so," replied Rock.

"Wow, he must be cold and hungry," said Robbie.

"Yes, but hopefully, we'll get him out today."

"Wait a minute," said Jack, "Aren't we forgetting about the clunkers?"

"Yes, what happens if they start bashing our boats?" said Charlie.

"All you have to do is feed coins into their heads."

"Can we use the coins we've got and if we can, how many will we need? Also, won't our coins be smaller than the coins the big'uns use?" asked Charlie.

"You'll be fine; our spies have paid clunkers with our coins and they like them. They keep them for themselves. They say that they are prettier than big'un coins."

"Are you saying that the clunkers can speak?" said Maggie.

"Did I forget to tell you that?" said Rooty.

"You've forgotten to tell us quite a bit, haven't you, Rooty?" said Jack, sounding angry.

"Some things have slipped my mind, that's true, but hopefully, you know everything now."

"If we can pay the clunkers, why do we need two elves to escort us?" said Sophie.

"In case of any unforeseen problems," said Rooty.

"Like what?" asked Charlie.

"We don't know of anything," said Rooty, "But these two elves," he pointed to the two elves who had guarded the doors when the children met the King and Queen. The taller-than-average elves stepped forward. They were now dressed all in black and both carried a sword, spear and bow and arrows. They looked quite fierce. "They are here just in case."

"Hello," they said together.

Freddie shouted, "They're twins!"

"Yes, we are," said the one on the left, "My name is Thorn and my brother here is Stinger."

"Hello," said Stinger.

"Wow," said Freddie, "We've now got three sets of twins!"

"Are you soldiers?" asked Lauren and Sam together.

Freddie snorted.

"Yes, we are sometimes," said Stinger, "Other times, we do different jobs."

"OK," said Rooty, "I think we need to get going."

Chapter 15

All the time the children and Rooty and Rock were talking, the hogsman elves had been harnessing the hogs and moles together. They stood in two rows of six, four moles at the front with four rows of two hogs behind. Trailing behind them were the ropes. The boats were side by side near the top of the tunnel. They looked very much like boats.

"OK," said Rooty, "Let's do one last check. Charlie and Maggie, have you both got your backpacks, bean lights, tree beans, compasses and money?"

"Yes," said Charlie, "We've divided the coins between us."

"We've done the same," said Maggie.

"Take these extra coins, just in case," said Rooty. He passed a bag to each group. "There's twenty coins in each bag. Hopefully, you won't need them."

The hogsman elves had attached the ropes to the back of the three boats. There was a lot of rope.

"Right," said Rooty, "Let's get you all in your boats."

The children got into their two groups and climbed into the boats. Each of the children's boats had two pairs of seats and four paddles. There was one seat at the back with a paddle for steering.

Thorn and Stinger's boat was a bit different. It only had one seat and two paddles.

The warning sign was taken down and the digger elves started to push the three boats onto the downward slope.

"Good luck," said Rooty and Rock. A big cheer went up from the rest of the gathered elves.

Slowly, the boats began to slide downwards; the digger elves let the rope slip through their little hands, keeping enough of a grip to stop the boats from going too fast.

The children all put on their bean lights, pushed tree beans onto the spikes and suddenly the tunnel was lit up but there was not much to see. Thorn and Stinger had hats on that lit up just as Rooty's had done.

After several minutes, the bottom of the tunnel could be seen and the water was beginning to react to the light from the bean lights.

The boats slowly slid onto the water. They were beautifully made and sat steadily on the water. All of the children and Thorn and Stinger studied the bottoms of their boats, checking for leaks. The two elves looked very worried but seemed encouraged by the reaction of the children.

"Are your boats OK?" called Charlie.

"Ours is OK," said Jack.

"Our boat doesn't have any water in it, which is good, isn't it?" asked Thorn.

"The shiny coating on the outside seems to be doing the job," said Charlie.

Suddenly, a voice boomed out, "Who's that, I can see lights, who are you? I'm stuck. Mum, Dad, is that you?"

"It's BigBum," said Maggie.

"Should we answer him?" asked Sophie.

"I can't see anything; where are the compasses?" asked Billy.

Charlie and Maggie had them in their backpacks. They quickly got them out.

"Where did Rooty say they thought BigBum might be?" asked Billy.

"To the west," said Charlie."

Just at that moment, a flock of silent light moths came out of the tunnel. They were glowing bright blue and immediately the lake could be seen clearly. The water glowed in reaction to their blueness; the lake was huge and the ceiling of the cave was about fifty feet above the surface of the water and sparkled like the night sky.

"Wow," Nearly everyone said at the same time.

Charlie and Maggie checked their compasses. They both pointed in the direction that the compasses indicated was west.

"That way," they said.

Everyone looked west.

"Can anyone see anything?" said Jack.

"Yes, I can see a big head sticking above the water," said Stinger.

"Yes, there he is," said both sets of twins.

"I can't see him," said Freddie.

"I can," said Charlie, "Look, he's there." He pointed again.

The voice called out again, "Who are you? You aren't my mum and dad!"

"We're here to help you," called Jack.

"I've been 'ere ages, I'm stuck. Are you little 'umans? You won't get me out!"

"We've got a plan; will you let us help you?" called Charlie.

"Yes, can we come over to you?" shouted Maggie.

"Alright, but I don't think you'll be able to get me out," shouted the young giant.

"We're coming now," shouted back Charlie.

Everybody started paddling and began making good progress. Even Thorn and Stinger were doing well; although, they did not look very happy and were concentrating really hard.

"Come on, Thorn, come on, Stinger," encouraged Sophie. "You're doing really well."

The three boats were about halfway to BigBum when suddenly, both the children's boats got bashed.

"Oh no," said Robbie. "It's the clunkers."

Everyone stopped paddling and started looking around.

'ery slowly, five silver fish faces appeared.

'as hard to judge how long their bodies were but to the

'he fish's heads were about the size of horses' heads.

They did not look vicious; in fact, they seemed to be smiling. "We're willing to pay, we've got elf money," said Maggie.

"Elf money?" said two of the fish at the same time.

"Do you think they're twins?" said Freddie.

"Shush," said Charlie to his brother.

"We like elf money, but what are you young humans doing here?"

"We've come to rescue a young big'un; he's trapped over there," said Jack, pointing towards BigBum.

"Yes, we've seen him, he's really stuck," said a clunker who sounded like a lady.

"We are going to pull him out using these ropes," said Robbie, holding up a rope. "They are connected to bighogs and moles up that tunnel. When we've secured them to the big'un, we'll give a signal and they will pull him out."

"Well, that sounds as if it might work," said the clunker who seemed to be the leader.

"All you have to do is pay us two elf coins for each of you young humans and five coins each for those two fierce-looking elves. This is the first time we've seen humans or big elves."

"OK," said Charlie, "That's 30 coins. If we say 35, that's seven coins for each of you, do you agree?"

"Very generous," said the clunker leader, "What's your name, young human?"

"Me—I'm Charlie—what's your name?"

"I'm Dart," said the clunker.

"OK," Charlie said to the others, "Give me your coins and I'll pay."

All the coins were passed to Charlie. "Right. If you swim alongside me one at a time, I'll pay you."

The clunkers formed a line and waited.

Charlie placed the coins in the slots on the top of the fish's heads. Each one said 'thank you' after being paid.

"Will you stay with us while we attempt to free the big'un?" said Charlie.

"We will," said Dart, "and if any nippers turn up, we'll get rid of them for you."

"Er, what are nippers?" asked Jack.

"They are nasty little creatures who bite anything moving in the water. But not us or giants," said Dart.

Jack turned to Thorn and Stinger. "Is this why elves are afraid of water?"

"Most elves are but we are not," said Thorn.

"But you know they exist, those nipper things?"

"Yes, we do but we didn't know they are in this lake."

"Ever since we've been involved in this adventure, we've constantly been told that we wouldn't be in danger, but now it seems we could be," said Charlie.

"You'll be alright as long as you don't go in the water and we don't see any reason that you will. Nippers are small and you will be safe in the boats."

"We'll stay with you," said Dart, "Nippers are afraid of us so we'll protect you. You've paid us well."

"We'll protect you too," said Stinger.

The children all looked at each other, not sure of what to do or say.

"Oi!" boomed BigBum's voice. "I thought you said you were going to 'elp me get unstuck."

"Yes, we are," said Jack, taking charge. "Come on everyone, start paddling."

The little group of children, elves and clunkers made their way slowly across the lake. The clunkers continually swam round the boats, keeping watch for nippers.

Dart's head slowly popped up. "There are quite a few nippers in here but they're keeping their distance," he said.

"Good," said the elves.

"Yes, keep them away please," said Sophie, "and thanks."

Chapter 16

When the children got about ten metres from BigBum, they stopped paddling. Although they could only see his head, he was obviously big. His head was about the size of a lorry wheel and he had lots of curly brown hair.

"What's your name?" called Charlie.

"We know his name," said Freddie.

"I'm being polite," said Charlie, "He might have a proper name."

"I'm BigBum 'cos I've got a big bum."

"Pleased to meet you," said Charlie.

"We're going to come closer and if you lift your hands out of the water, we will attach ropes around your wrists."

"You're not going to tie me up!" shouted BigBum. A big hand came out of the water and splashed back down. All three boats rocked back and forth. The children and elves held on tightly.

"No wait," shouted Charlie, "We're not going to tie you up. All we will do is loop the ropes round your wrists and then pull you out. If you look, there's a tunnel over there; can you see the light?"

"Yes, I can see it."

"Well, the ropes go up there and the ends are connected to a team of creatures who will pull you out."

"I'm quite big; do you think your creatures are strong enough?"

"There are twelve creatures up there.
I'm sure they are strong enough," replied Charlie.

"Alright then, I'll let you do it."

"OK, lift your hands up." The young giant lifted his hands up just above the water; they were very big hands. "We'll have to make the loops a lot bigger," said Robbie.

Sophie and Maggie explained what was happening while the boys adjusted the ropes. "Right, BigBum, point your fingers towards us."

He did as he was told and very carefully, the two boats of children paddled nearer and very slowly slid the ropes over his hands.

"Now if you hold onto the ropes, they won't slip off."

"What, like this?" said BigBum.

"That's perfect," said Sophie and she patted his hand.

BigBum gave a big toothy grin.

"Hold tight, BigBum," shouted Charlie, "Give the signal Jack.

Jack gave a loud blast. BigBum looked terrified and he immediately clamped his big hands over his ears. This caused the ropes to go tight. Unfortunately, one of the ropes was under the boat that contained Maggie, Emma, Charlie, Freddie and Robbie. The rope rocked the boat right over and the children fell into the lake. One by one, they popped up, except Freddie.

"Where's Freddie?" shouted Charlie in panic.

"I can't see him; where is he?" Maggie screamed.

Everyone was looking around the boats. "Freddie! Freddie!" they all shouted. Suddenly, Freddie's head popped up followed by the rest of his body. The children were all amazed to see him sitting on the back of Dart.

"Wow," said Freddie, "You've saved me, Dart. I couldn't get my bearings; I didn't know which way was up and then you came and slid underneath me and up we went. Thank you."

"That's OK, it was all a bit confusing, I must admit. Is everybody else safe?" asked Dart.

"Yes, we are all OK, thanks Dart," said Charlie. They all climbed back into their boat.

"Look," said Lauren pointing at BigBum. He still had his hands over his ears and his eyes were tightly shut.

"How can we get him to open his eyes?" said Lauren and Sam together.

"I know," said Thorn, giving BigBum a slight prod with his spear. BigBum opened one eye and looked around, opened the other eye and saw all the others. He took his hands down.

"What was that noise?" he asked.

"Sorry," said Jack, "That was the signal and look, the ropes are going tight, can you feel it, BigBum?"

"Yes, I can."

"Then hold on," said Jack. "This is it. Grip the ropes again." The children quickly paddled the boats to one side. The ropes got tighter. BigBum's arms began stretching out in front of him.

Up in the tunnel and beyond, the ropes were getting really tight. The hogmen were shouting encouragement to the hogs and moles. They leant into their harness and dug their claws into the ground. They were huffing and puffing. It seemed as though the plan was not working. Then all the gathered elves started cheering and shouting, "Pull, pull, pull." Very slowly, the hogs and moles started moving. One step after another, they moved forwards. "It's working!" shouted Rooty, slapping Rock on the back.

Back on the lake, everyone was looking at the ropes and then at Bigbum. His face was going redder and redder; his knuckles were white where he was gripping the rope tightly.

"It's not working," he said, "It's not working!"

"Keep holding on," shouted three sets of twins.

Back in the chamber, all of the elves who could pull, were heaving on the ropes, helping the hogs and moles. "Pull, pull," shouted the hogmen, "Come on, we can do it."

On the lake, bubbles, tiny bubbles, started appearing on the surface. "Ooer," said BigBum, "something is happening." Suddenly, BigBum's shoulders started to appear, then his chest and he popped out of the water like a cork, causing a huge splash which upset all three boats. Everyone was thrown into the water. "I'm free, I'm free!" shouted BigBum.

Everything was a mess, children, elves and boats all around. "Help us, Bigbum," shouted Charlie.

"What's up?" he replied, "Crikey, what are you doing in the water?"

"It doesn't matter but please help us."

The young giant quickly slipped the ropes from his wrists and held his hands out flat. "Hold onto my fingers," said BigBum, "One of you on each finger."

"Quick everyone, hang on," said Charlie.

All of the children grabbed a finger or thumb and held on tightly. "Where are Thorn and Stinger?" asked Sophie. "I can't see them."

"Look over there," said Maggie, pointing. The other children looked over to one side and there were the two elves, looking terrified but safely sitting on the back of a clunker each.

Dart's head popped up. "We didn't think the elves would be comfortable being rescued by a giant so we decided we would help them. Fortunately, with all the splashing, the nippers swam away."

"Our friends are keeping them at a distance."

"What do we do now?" asked Freddie.

"Let's try to get back into the boats," suggested Billy.

"Wait a minute," said Jack, "The ropes are still being pulled. We need them to get back up the tunnel."

Thorn suddenly spoke up, "Dart, can you take me and Stinger over to the tunnel and we'll shout up to stop pulling?"

"Good idea," said Dart and sent the two clunkers dashing off with the two elves clinging on desperately.

"Look," said Lauren pointing, "You can see a lot more of BigBum now."

"You're right," said Maggie, "The water is definitely getting lower."

"Come on quick, let's get in the boats," said Robbie.

"Where are they?" said Freddie.

"There's one just the other side of BigBum's arm," said Sam.

"And another," said Emma.

"I can only see those two," said Charlie, "and they are ours. Thorn's and Stinger's boat must have sunk."

"I'll take a look," said Dart, slipping under the water.

"BigBum, can you move us nearer to our boats please?" said Maggie.

"I don't like calling him that," said Freddie, "Can't we call him something else?"

"What about just 'Big'?" suggested Billy and Sophie together.

"I know," said Robbie, "What about 'BB'?"

"I like it," said Charlie. Everyone agreed.

"OK," said Freddie, "Let's ask him."

"Go ahead," said Charlie, "You ask him, Freddie."

"Er, excuse me, BigBum?" said Freddie.

"I heard what you were talking about. I may be big but I'm not deaf," he replied, "If you want to, you can call me 'BB', it sounds quite good actually."

"BB it is then," said Charlie.

"Right, let's get you all back in your boats," said BB.

The children all scrambled back into the two remaining boats. At that moment, Dart reappeared. "I'm afraid the elves' boat is on the bottom of the lake in two pieces."

"Do you realise you are standing on the lake bed?" he asked the young giant.

"Oh yes, I am, I didn't notice."

"I think we should start moving towards the tunnel," said Maggie.

"You're right," said Jack. "The only problem is that we don't seem to have any paddles."

"Not to worry," said BB, "I'll push you." He started gently pushing the two boats towards the other side of the lake.

Chapter 17

Thorn and Stinger had arrived at the tunnel but because the water level had dropped, the entrance hole was too high for them to climb in.

"What shall we do, brother?" said Stinger.

"I hope some elf at the top will hear us when we start shouting," said Thorn.

One of the clunkers that the elves were sitting on spoke up, "Can either of you make the noise that the boy Jack made?" she asked.

"I don't know, we've never tried," said Thorn, "How did he do it?"

"He put his fingers in his mouth somehow and blew," said Stinger.

"What, like this?" Thorn said, putting his fingers in.

'Flurp' was the only noise that came out. Stinger laughed.

"OK clever," said Thorn, "You try."

'Fweep'

"Try again," encouraged Thorn. "That wasn't bad."

Stinger tried again and again, each time getting better. Then on the next try, he let out a loud shrill whistle.

"Well done, Stinger!" said both the clunkers (they were twins too).

"Yes, that was great," said Thorn, "Let's hope some elf heard it."

They waited and waited a bit longer. "Who's there?" came a voice from the tunnel.

"Thorn and Stinger."

Two silent lights fluttered into view. An elf appeared in the light. He was dressed exactly like the brothers. "Is that you, Barb?" asked Stinger.

"Yes, it's me," said Barb, "Still looking after my little brothers as usual."

The clunkers said, "You're all brothers then?"

"We are and who are you?"

"We are Ariana and Rita," replied both clunkers.

"Thanks for all your help," said Thorn.

"We've enjoyed it all," said Rita.

"Will we be able to climb up the ropes to get to you, Barb?" asked Stinger. "Are they secured at the top or are we likely to sink into the water?"

"Once we heard the second signal, the ropes were secured to stakes so you should be OK."

"Good," said Stinger, "I've had enough of being wet."

The water was getting lower, which made the climb to the tunnel entrance about ten feet. Ariana and Rita moved closer to the ropes and the elf brothers grabbed a rope each and began climbing up.

Barb suddenly let out a cry. "There's a big'un heading this way; he's very big and he's pushing the children's boats in front of him."

"That's the big'un who was stuck; we managed to free him," said Thorn, pointing.

"He's got a big smile on his face, he looks really happy," said Stinger, climbing over the edge of the tunnel entrance.

"I never thought I'd see a big'un close up," said Barb, "Is he safe with the children?"

"Yes, he seems to be pretty friendly; he helped the children after they all fell into the water," said Thorn.

"Didn't he help you too?" asked Barb.

"He didn't need to; Ariana and Rita came to the rescue," Thorn said, waving at the two clunkers.

"We'd better get back to scaring the nippers away," said Ariana. "They seem to be getting a bit braver."

"OK, thanks for your help," said Thorn and Stinger at the same time.

The clunkers disappeared below the surface just as the boats came up to the ropes. More of BB was now visible; he was indeed very big.

"Thanks, BB," shouted Freddie.

The elf twins looked at each other and both said, "BB?"

"Yeah, thanks BB, we'll climb up from here," said Jack.

"No need to," said BB. "Climb onto my hand two at a time and I'll lift you up."

"OK, thanks." The children climbed onto BB's open hand and he gently moved them two at a time to the tunnel entrance.

They all turned to face the young giant.

Charlie stepped forward. "I think we are all pleased to have been able to get you unstuck, BB, and we're all pleased to have met you. You're a nice big'un. Perhaps, we'll meet again one day."

"I'd like that very much. I don't know why 'umans and big'uns don't get on. You all seem very nice to me and that includes your friends, the elves."

Sophie and Emma went forward and each of them patted BB on his big fingers. "You're lovely," they said at the same time.

"Oh no," said Freddie, "not more twins." Everyone laughed except BB and Barb who did not get the joke.

Dart suddenly popped into view. "We've got a problem—the tunnel that BB used to get here doesn't seem to be emptying."

"Does that mean the tunnel is blocked?" asked BB.

"We think so; Ariana and Rita have gone down to investigate, they should be back soon."

"How will BB get back home if the tunnel is blocked?" asked Freddie in a worried voice.

"Are there any other tunnels that go down to Bigland, Dart?" asked Charlie.

"Not that we know of," replied Dart. "We only found this one because one of our friends saw BB disappearing up it. It was hidden behind some trees. Being inquisitive, we formed a search party to see where it led."

The two girl clunkers pushed their heads up. "The bottom end of the tunnel is blocked by big rocks," said Ariana. "It must have been blocked from outside."

"Why would the big'uns have blocked it up?" said Robbie.

"Perhaps, there was so much water going down the tunnel, it was causing a problem. The only thing is that they didn't know BB was stuck up in the lake. What do you think?" said Maggie.

"That sounds like it could be true," said Charlie.

"I could swim down the tunnel and bash the rocks out," said BB.

"I don't think you'd be able to do it," said Rita, "It looks really hard."

"What can we do to help BB?" said Freddie.

"Has anyone got an idea?" asked Jack.

Everyone stood thinking.

Freddie spoke up first, "Couldn't your elf spies somehow get a message to the big'uns telling them what's happened?"

"It would be very dangerous," said Thorn, "The big'uns don't like us elves."

"Yes, we know that," said Charlie.

"What about writing a message, tying it to an arrow and firing it into the big'un King's palace?" suggested Freddie.

"That's a brilliant idea, Freddie," said his big brother.

"Do you think it could be done, Thorn?" asked Charlie.

"We could do it, I suppose," said Thorn, "But we'd have to get permission from King Bigfists."

The children had now been joined by Rooty, Rock and Norris. "What's the delay?" asked Rooty who suddenly caught sight of BB. "Crikey," said Rooty, "He's a big one, isn't he? Is he OK?"

"Yes, he's OK but he's wet and very hungry," said Sophie.

Rooty sent Rock back up the tunnel to organise some food, a lot of food, for the young giant.

Charlie and the others then told Rooty about the tunnel being blocked. They told him of Freddie's plan.

Rooty said he thought it was a good plan and set off to get permission from the King. The three elf brothers went with him.

After about 30 minutes, several carts were lowered down the slope to the children. The carts were full of food. Huge pots of porridge, giant loaves of bread, lots of vegetables and fruits. They pushed the carts to the front of the tunnel.

"Here you are, BB, it's all for you."

"That's very kind of you," said BB and started eating.

The children were all surprised how delicately BB ate the food. They expected him to wolf it down in big mouthfuls but he gently picked up small bits in his big finger and thumb.

Sophie nudged Maggie who was standing beside her. "Look Maggie," she said, "I think BB's got tears in his eyes."

"Oh yes, he has," replied Maggie.

Sophie walked towards BB. "BB," she whispered, "are you OK?"

"I'm very OK, thanks," he said. "It's just so nice that you are being so kind to me. I didn't think 'umans and elves were nice."

"Well, we didn't think giants were nice, but you are," said Sophie.

"Thank you," said BB. "How can I repay you?"

"Just tell all your people that we don't want to be enemies, just friends," said Maggie.

"I will if I ever get back home."

Just then Rooty and Rock returned. "The King has given us permission," said Rooty. "Thorn and his brothers have volunteered to go down and meet our spies. They will show them where to fire their arrows. They are on their way now."

"Have you written the messages?" asked Robbie.

"Yes," said Rock, "Queen Blush wrote them herself. One for each of the brothers. They are all excellent shots with bows and arrows. We decided to send the same message three times, to be on the safe side."

"What do the messages say?" asked Lauren.

"King Ralph, your son has been stranded in a lake. He has been rescued by some young humans and elves. To get him back home, you need to unblock the tunnel where the water was pouring out. Do it quickly; he wants to see his mum and dad.

He misses you."

"Let's hope they unblock it soon," said Lauren.

Charlie shouted to BB, "Did you hear that, BB, the message will get to your mum and dad soon."

"Thank you all. I can see a ledge over there," he pointed a big finger, "I'll climb up there and wait for the water to go down my tunnel."

Some elves were left to keep watch. Everyone else went back up to the chamber to get dry and grab something to eat. And wait.

Chapter 18

Thorn, Stinger and Barb stopped at the bottom of the spy tunnel. The entrance was covered by bushes. Thorn risked a quick look outside: he did not see much, only trees and grass and more bushes. He ducked his head back inside. Suddenly, two small figures stepped into the dark entrance—both were dressed in black—two elf spies!

"Welcome to Big Land," said one of the spies, "My name is Ash and this is Berry, my sister."

Barb stepped forward. "I know you, Ash, we trained together, didn't we?"

"Yes Barb, we did," said Ash.

"Yes, and we know Berry, we were at school together," said Stinger.

"We didn't know you are spies," said Barb.

"Yes, well, it's supposed to be a secret. It helps in our line of work," said Berry.

"Yes, of course," said Thorn, "Nice to see you again, Berry."

"And you, Thorn," replied the girl spy.

"The young big'un—BB—says they know about our spies," said Thorn.

"We know, we play a game of cat and mouse down here but they haven't caught any of us yet," said Ash.

"If we're going to reunite BB with his family, we'd better get on with our mission," said Barb.

"Yes, how far is it to King Ralph's palace?" asked Stinger.

"It's not really a palace, more like a big wooden house. It's quite nice though," said Berry.

"It's not too far actually," said Ash, "Once we get past the trees, you'll be able to see it."

"Are we likely to meet any big'uns?" asked Barb.

"Not this time of day; they all seem to take naps about now. Come on, let's go," said Ash.

For the next half an hour, the five elves made their way to Ralph's house. They only saw one big'un who was awake. The big'uns seemed to nap wherever they wanted. Leaning against trees, lying on the ground, some were even asleep standing up leaning against each other.

The walls of the houses were massive, almost like cliffs to the elves.

There were several guards around the big house but like all the other big'uns, they were sleeping.

"We'd better get higher up so that we can see through a window," said Ash.

All five elves climbed up a nearby tree. They could see through a big open window. Ralph the Massive was asleep with his head on his arms on a table. Queen Very Loud was asleep on a sofa.

"Look," said Thorn, "There's a wooden goblet just beside Ralph's head. I think I could easily hit it and with any luck, it might knock it over."

"OK," said Barb, "Where should we place the other arrows?"

"What about in the shield of that guard on the right of the main door? I could easily hit that," said Stinger.

"OK, that leaves me," said Barb, "Where should I put my arrow?"

"How good are you?" asked Berry.

"He's the best," said Thorn and Stinger at the same time.

"Do you think you could hit the rope holding the bell outside the door?"

"I could but it would take several arrows to cut it," said Barb.

"OK, when you start trying to cut it, Thorn and Stinger, you be ready when the bell falls to fire your arrows. Hopefully, the noise will wake up the King and Queen and they will see the messages."

"That's a good plan, Berry," said Ash, "Although I think we should leave straight away after the bell falls and the other arrows are on their way."

"Let's do it," said Barb.

He took careful aim and fired his first arrow. They all watched as the arrow nicked the bell rope.

"Good shot," said Berry.

Barb fired three more arrows and each one caught the rope. The bell still hung from its fixing. Another two shots and they could all see the rope was fraying.

"Keep going, Barb," said the twins.

He fired two more arrows.

"Look," said Ash, "it's starting to unravel."

The rope was indeed coming apart, the strands were spinning round and the bell was wobbling.

"One more should do it, get your arrows ready."

The three brothers loaded the arrows with the messages attached; Barb fired his arrow and his brothers held their bows ready. They all held their breath as the arrow sped towards the rope. With a loud twang, the rope snapped and dropped. It hit one of the guards on the head. The other arrows were already on their way.

Thorn's arrow thwacked into the goblet and knocked it over, splashing King Ralph with what looked like wine.

"Whah!" roared Ralph, "Who did this?" The Queen woke up screaming.

"Did you do that?" shouted Ralph to his wife.

"What?" shouted the Queen in a very loud voice.

"Knock my drink all over me."

"How could I have? I was asleep over here."

"Well, someone must have; look, it's tipped over."

The Queen peered at the goblet. "What's that sticking in it?"

Ralph picked up his goblet. "Well, I'll be—it's an elf arrow," he exclaimed.

With his big finger and thumb, he easily pulled the arrow out. "There's something tied round it," said the Queen, snatching it away. "It's a message; where are my glasses, it's so small."

Ralph found the Queen's glasses and pushed them across the table to her. She read the message. "The elves have found our boy—he's safe!" she bellowed.

By this time, the elfin group were racing back to safety. "Sounds like they've found a note," Ash said, half-laughing.

Big'uns were everywhere but they all seemed to be heading for the King's house. No one was looking for them yet. All the elves had to do was avoid the large feet crashing about.

In the royal house, the guard was showing the message to the King and Queen.

"Yes, we already know; we've got one too," screeched the Queen.

"Do you know where this tunnel is?" asked the King.

"Yes Sire," answered the guard, "I was one of a group of men ordered to block the tunnel. The water that was coming out was flooding the royal kitchens. It was a difficult job to block the tunnel but we managed to do it."

"Why was I not told of this?" roared King Ralph.

"I don't know," said the guard.

The main door was opened by another big'un. This man was the King's most senior guard.

"We thought it was not important enough to bother you with, sir."

"I decide what is important, and what is important now is to unblock that tunnel so that our son can come home. Get the men together and get it unblocked now," shouted Ralph.

"Yes Sir," said the guard.

The senior guard ran off to carry out the King's order. He organised a group of ten big'un guards. They made their way to the blocked tunnel entrance. Within 45 minutes of King Ralph being woken up, the guards were huffing and puffing, trying to dislodge the rocks that had so carefully been placed there only a few days before.

At about the same time, the elves had reached the spy tunnel entrance.

There was another elf dressed in black waiting for them.

"Hello Newt," said Ash, "Why are you here?"

"To find out if you were successful; were you?"

"Yes, we were, sure we were," said Barb.

"Good," said Newt, picking up a small drum.

"What are you doing?" asked Thorn.

"We've set up a team of drummers along the tunnel so the news will be sent quicker this way," said Newt. He beat a quick series of bangs on his drum.

"How will they know that the drumbeats mean that we did it?" asked Berry.

"It's the only message we are to send," replied Newt.

The elves could hear the drumbeats being repeated up the tunnel, slowly getting fainter.

Chapter 19

In the chamber up above the lake, everyone was sitting around waiting for news. Suddenly, Sky, the speedy bighog, dashed into the chamber. Clinging to her spiny back was another spy elf.

"They did it," she shouted.

A great cheer echoed all around as elves and children jumped about, smiling and laughing.

"Quick," called Charlie. "We've got to let BB know."

All the children and Rooty and Rock made their way down to the bottom of the tunnel.

"BB," shouted Charlie, "the message got through."

"That's good but the water is still in the tunnel," BB said.

Dart had been listening. "I'll swim down and see what's happening at the bottom of BB's tunnel."

"OK Dart, but be careful."

He disappeared into the water. Everyone waited.

"Don't worry, BB," called Sophie. "You'll be home soon."

"I hope so, I want to see my mum and dad," said the young big'un.

"BB?" said Maggie.

"Yes," he replied.

"How old are you?"

"I'm ten."

"We humans are all ten too."

"I'm not," said Freddie, "I'm only eight."

Jack turned to Robbie, "He's just a kid like us."

"Yeah," said Robbie, "but about ten times bigger."

Dart's head popped back up. "There's lots of banging at the bottom of the tunnel," he said. "They must be very busy on the other side of the blockage."

"Look," said Freddie, "something's happening."

They looked over to the tunnel top; fish were leaping out of the water.

"That's the nippers," said Dart. "They must be trying to stop being pulled down by the water. They must have unblocked it down there!"

Sure enough, they could see that the tunnel top was now completely exposed.

"BB look, you can see that the water is disappearing down the tunnel, you can go home!" shouted Sophie.

BB jumped off the ledge, the water now only up to his waist. He waded towards his tunnel. Halfway there, he stopped and turned round.

"Thank you all for saving me, you are all very nice; perhaps, one day we'll see each other again. Bye."

He waded on to the tunnel top, turned round again, waved then turned back and dived down the tunnel.

"Wow," said Freddie.

"He's gone," said Sophie, Billy, Thorn and Stinger at the same time. "Will he be OK going headfirst?"

"I don't know," said Charlie.

"I'll go and take a look," called Dart, speeding off towards the tunnel.

Everyone stood watching.

Dart clambered up to the tunnel entrance and slithered from sight.

"Will he be able to get back up?" asked Lauren.

"That's the way he came here in the first place, walking on his fins, so I think he'll be OK," said Robbie.

The other clunkers had swum over to wait for Dart. They did not have to wait very long. Dart's head suddenly appeared and he flopped back into the lake.

He popped back up. "I only had to go halfway. I could hear cheering and shouting from the bottom; I think he made it!"

Once again, the children and elves all started clapping and cheering.

The children, elves, bighogs and moles made their way from the lake chamber back to the main elf area.

Rooty, Rock, Norris and Barb left the rest and went to report to the King and Queen.

The Rainbow Gang made their way to their dormitory.

They all flopped onto their beds.

"That was really fun," said Maggie.

"It really was," said Billy, Sophie, Lauren and Sam together.

Everyone laughed; of course, Freddie laughed longest.

"Have you looked at the mess we are in? Our clothes are creased and we all look bedraggled," said Charlie.

"You're right," said Robbie, "I think we'd better get cleaned up. Do you think we can put our clothes in for washing?"

A small head appeared around the kitchen door, it was a lady cook elf. "Of course you can," she said. "Go and get clean, put your clothes in the hatch and the cleaning elves will take care of them. While you do that, we'll prepare some hot food for you."

"Thanks very much," said Emma and Jack together.

Everyone looked at Freddie.

"What?" he asked.

"Nothing to say?" asked Charlie.

"Well, no, 'cos I know they aren't related," replied Freddie.

They all laughed again.

About an hour later, they were all bathed or showered and dressed in freshly washed clothes.

The door from the tunnel opened and the King and Queen stood in the doorway.

"May we come in?" asked Queen Blush.

"Of course," said Charlie.

The King and Queen came in. Behind them came Rooty, Rock and the three big elf brothers—Thorn, Stinger and Barb.

"We've come here to say thank you for all your hard work," said King Bigfists, "and to say that we are having a banquet tonight in your honour."

"It wasn't just us," said Charlie, "Lots of others made it all possible."

"Yes indeed, and we'll all be celebrating everyone's efforts. Humans, elves, animals and even fish," said the King.

"Thank you," said Maggie.

"We will see you all later," said Queen Blush.

The King and Queen left. Everyone started chatting and laughing. "A banquet," said Billy, "That's great."

"Is a banquet a party?" asked Freddie.

"Yes, with lots of people and lots to eat and drink," said Rock.

Later that evening, the children were escorted to the main chamber by Rooty and Rock. It was filled with tables surrounded by elves. King Bigfists and Queen Blush sat at a big table at the end. As the group of children entered, everyone stood up and clapped.

The children were led to an empty table in front of the King and Queen. They sat down, the King called for quiet, the clapping stopped and everyone sat down. The King remained standing.

"We are here tonight to celebrate the success we had today, releasing the young big'un, BigBum, who now goes by the name, BB. A much nicer name given to him by the youngsters sitting here in front of us. The Rainbow Gang, Norris and his diggers, Rooty, Rock and all the other elves. Especially those who went to Bigland and the elves who led the way. They know who they are. Also, our friends the hogs and moles and our new friends, the clunkers." Everyone clapped and cheered.

"Let the banquet begin!" shouted the King.

The Rainbow Gang and The Girls went to bed very late that night. They had had a wonderful time, meeting lots of elves and answering their many questions. They all ate loads of delicious food. They did not really know what it was but it was all fantastic.

In the morning, they all slept in. It was only when Rooty and Rock arrived that they began to wake up. They all got dressed and ate their breakfast.

When they had all finished, Rock said, "I suppose we'd better take you all home; collect your belongings and join us out in the tunnel."

Chapter 20

When they were ready, the children went through the doors. They could see a big hog with a cart strapped to it.

"It's Quill," shouted Freddie, "and Rock, Rooty and Conker."

"Hello," said Quill, "We are here to take you girls back to your up-and-down."

"Oh," said Charlie, "We can walk to our up-and-down, can't we?"

"We've got to say goodbye then," said Maggie.

"Yes, but we'll see you soon, won't we?" said Sophie.

"Of course, it only takes half an hour or so on the bus, doesn't it? I'll phone you, Sophie."

"Now we've got each other's numbers, we'll get together often," replied Sophie.

"Climb aboard," said Conker. The girls got into the cart.

"See you soon," said Maggie.

"Bye," said Lauren and Sam.

Emma was crying so she just waved.

"Let's go, Quill," said Conker and off they went. The Rainbow Gang stood watching until the girls were out of sight.

They all set off up the tunnel.

At the up-and-down, Rooty said, "Right. Charlie, Freddie and Jack, you go up first with Rock."

They climbed onto the platform and after a short while, they were at the top.

"Wait while I check to see whether it's safe to go out." Rock took something out of his pocket which looked like a round mirror.

"What's that?" asked Freddie.

"It can look outside so I can see whether there is anyone," said Rock.

"Can I have a go?" said Freddie.

Rock passed it to him. Freddie held it flat on his hand. "Now turn around," said Rock.

Freddie did as he was told. "I can see all around the tree; it's like there is a periscope at the top," he said.

"I don't know what a periscope is, but this is magic," said Rock. The others all had a go with the magic mirror.

"Come on, let's go," said Rock.

He pulled a lever and the door opened.

They all stepped out. Rock pushed the door back into place.

"We'll wait here for the others," said Rock and within a couple of seconds, the door opened and the rest stepped out. They looked all around, no one was there. Rock reached into his pocket again and took out a small red bag. He threw it on the ground. There was a puff of red mist and suddenly all the bikes were there.

"I'm sure we'll meet again," said Rooty.

"I hope so," said Jack.

"Me too," said the twins.

"Thanks for a great adventure," said Charlie.

"Yeah, it was fun," said Robbie.

"We'll miss you," said Freddie.

"We'll miss you too," said Rooty and Rock at the same time. They climbed back into the tree, the door closed and they were gone.

"You don't think—" said Freddie.

"What, that they are twins? Who knows," said Charlie, "They might be."

"I've just checked the time; it's just like it was before we went into the tree," said Jack.

"Wow!" said Freddie.

"That's really weird," said Robbie, "We must have been gone for at least two days but here it's as if time has stood still."

"Well, it's magic, isn't that what Rooty told us?" said Sophie.

"It must be," said Jack, "There's no other explanation, is there?"

"So what's the time now?" asked Charlie.

"It's five past four," replied Jack.

"So we've still got nearly an hour before our mums and dads are expecting us. Can we go and see if we can speak to Chester?" said Billy.

"Great idea," said Charlie, "Come on, let's go."

The group of friends got on their bikes and rode across the park to Charlie and Freddie's garden. Charlie unlocked the gate and they all went in.

Freddie pointed at the shed and said, "What's that light, Charlie? Dad hasn't got a light in his shed."

The other children stopped and looked and there was definitely a blue light coming from inside the shed.

"That's funny; Dad has said for ages that he was going to put a light in there but he hasn't done it yet," said Charlie.

"Perhaps he's done it while we've been away," suggested Freddie.

"But we haven't been away; time hasn't moved since we were down with the elves, remember?" said Billy.

"Oh yeah," replied Freddie, "Come on, Charlie, unlock the door and let's have a look."

Charlie unlocked the door and held it wide open. The children could not believe their eyes. The chest was in the middle of the floor and sitting on it was a tall elf, a blue glowing elf. Nobody moved or spoke.

"Hello kids," said the elf. "It's me, Chester—well, not really me. This is what I believe you call a hologram."

Still no one said anything; most of the children just had their mouths open. Sophie was the first to speak, "So is this what you really look like?"

"Yes, but not blue," said Chester.

"Why haven't you appeared like this before?" asked Charlie.

"We've only just discovered how to do it. We didn't have the technology, but now we have and it works!"

"So who's here?"

They all introduced themselves. "Can you see us?" asked Jack.

"Yes, I can; some of this is technology, the rest is magic," replied Chester.

"Wow," said Freddie, "this is great."

"You all did a great job rescuing BB, as I believe you've renamed the young giant, and the water is flowing properly again. Well done. You can have a rest now."

"Thanks, Chester," said Charlie. "Although we all got really wet, we had a fantastic time."

"Yes, meeting Maggie and the other girls was great," said Sophie.

"Don't forget all the elves and hogs and moles and BB," said Freddie.

"If we go on another adventure, can the girls come too?" asked Sophie.

"We'll have to see," said Chester. "I'd like to think so. You make a great team."

"Thanks again," said Billy and Sophie together.

Of course, Freddie giggled.

"Do you know about how twins say the same things, Chester?" asked Freddie.

"As a matter of fact, I do; I have a twin sister called Magenta. That's a colour so she could be part of the Rainbow gang."

This information set all of the children asking loads of questions.

Freddie was so excited he could hardly speak.

After all the questions, Chester made an announcement.

"I think you'd all better get going home, you must be quite tired after all the adventure. Charlie and Freddie, just a word about the chest. Don't keep checking it. Your parents may get suspicious if you are always in this shed. Only check once a week. If there is anything I need to tell you about, you'll know."

"I'm going to go now," said Chester, "Thanks for all your help. We'll see each other soon, I'm sure. Bye."

"Bye," the children said.

The blue light disappeared and Chester was gone.

The chest moved to one side and became the boxes and tins again.

The Rainbow Gang sat quietly for a minute.

"That was brilliant," said Freddie. Everyone agreed and chatted excitedly for a few minutes and then decided to go to their homes.

"Shall we meet up tomorrow?" suggested Robbie.

They all agreed and left the shed and went off.

Charlie and Freddie waited at Billy's and Sophie's house until their mum and dad were in and then went home.

"Hello boys," said their dad, "How was your day?"

"OK," said Charlie, "The same as usual."

Freddie started smirking until Charlie glared at him.

"Yeah, same as usual, Dad," said Freddie, looking serious.

THE END